ELIZA'S JOURNAL

written by Caelyn Aß Williams ☾ illustrated by Kati Green

Library of Congress Catalog Number 2012940605
ISBN: 978-0-9844422-5-6

Art Director: Erica Melville
Cover and interior design by Brian David Smith
Cover illustrations by Kati Green

Printed in the United States of America

CRAIGMORE
CREATIONS

2900 SE Stark Street, Suite 1A
Portland, OR 97214
www.craigmorecreations.com

To my family and friends who have always been there for me, even from afar. To my Aunt, who encouraged me to attempt what I thought was impossible.

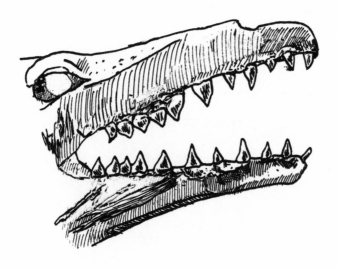

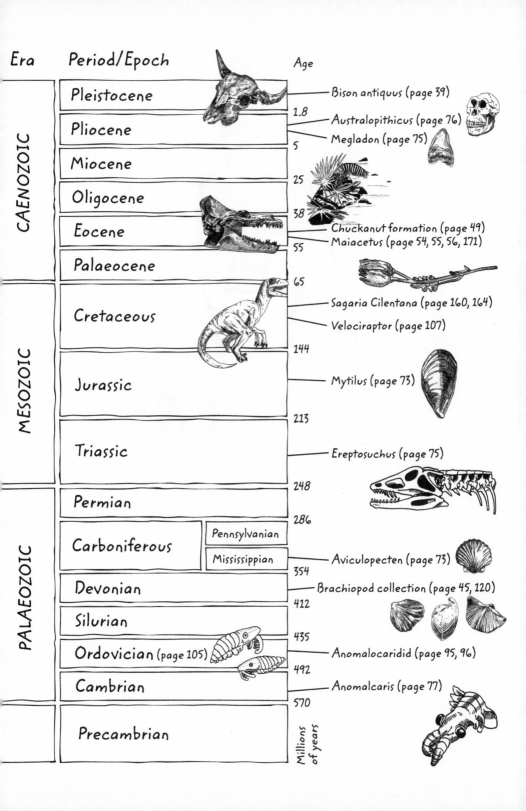

Era	Period/Epoch		Age
CAENOZOIC	Pleistocene		
	Pliocene		1.8
	Miocene		5
	Oligocene		25
	Eocene		38
	Palaeocene		55
MESOZOIC	Cretaceous		65
	Jurassic		144
	Triassic		213
PALAEOZOIC	Permian		248
	Carboniferous	Pennsylvanian	286
		Mississippian	
	Devonian		354
	Silurian		412
	Ordovician (page 105)		435
	Cambrian		492
	Precambrian		570

Millions of years

— Bison antiquus (page 39)

— Australopithicus (page 76)
— Megladon (page 75)

— Chuckanut formation (page 49)
— Maiacetus (page 54, 55, 56, 171)

— Sagaria Cilentana (page 160, 164)

— Velociraptor (page 107)

— Mytilus (page 73)

— Ereptosuchus (page 75)

— Aviculopecten (page 73)

— Brachiopod collection (page 45, 120)

— Anomalocaridid (page 95, 96)

— Anomalcaris (page 77)

Self-portrait

There are certain things that happen to one's sanity after long periods of time on a bus.

The older man in the row behind me has started to groan in mild agony. A few rows in front of me, a young man is bouncing his foot at such a rate I'm beginning to believe he's actually part jackrabbit. The girl sitting next to me keeps sighing and forlornly looking down at what appears to be a lock of hair in a Ziploc bag.

In my case, I've decided to start writing in the journal my mother gave me. If the battery on my iPod hadn't died two hours into the ride, I promise you, I wouldn't be writing now.

For a while I desperately attempted to draw in my sketchbook. I should have pieced together that bus + bumpy road = the bird I was trying to draw ending up looking more like a starfish. So, seeing as I have nothing else to do for the next… ugh, more time than I'd really like to imagine… I suppose I'll be writing here.

My name is Eliza E. Walcott, and I'm at the plus end of fifteen years old. I was born in San Francisco, but I've spent almost all of my life in Irvine, California. I live with my mother and father in a three-bedroom apartment complex. I'm sure we could've moved in to a house if we wanted, but my family needed to be downtown. And it saves on gas, I'm sure.

I have aunts and uncles and cousins, but none of them live very close. My Aunt Anna and her husband run a vineyard in El Dorado. I'd rather visit them, but my mother is of the opinion I have no place being in a vineyard all summer with little supervision.

Truth be told, I've never been connected to the rest of my family. It doesn't help that half of my mom's side of the family speaks Spanish. Sometimes I'll answer the phone to a lightning-quick Spanish voice, and I'll pass it to my mother who can actually speak it. But trust me, a call at 3:00 in the morning in Spanish is confusing when you've just woken up, especially when your grasp of the Spanish language consists of obscenities you learned watching your mother drive in traffic.

But it's my dad's side of the family I'll be dealing with all summer, which means as long as I can interpret my uncle's old-man grunts there won't be much of a language barrier. Except when it comes to technology. Last Thanksgiving I mentioned my iPod and Uncle Pat gave me a look like I was from Mars.

There's a reason (besides geography) I've never been very close with the man. The looks he gives me have always been the same. I highly doubt he's changed his sunny demeanor much in the last few years. I mean, he's a 50-something man and I'm a teenage girl. I talk about my last semester in school, and he talks about fishing in the barren, *soul crushing*, icy vastness of Alaska.

This is the man whose home I am speeding towards, into the evergreen north, in the San Juan Islands. For an entire summer.

To be fair, his wife, my Auntie Gin, is completely nice. I'm not entirely sure why those two married in the first place. Gin is warm and kind. She worked in an arts & crafts shop for a few years before teaching kindergarten. You have to have a really high tolerance level to work with little screaming children, and that probably carried over well in marrying a terse, grumpy guy.

But still, I'd rather be home, happily lounging around the house in my pajamas. Or at my art teacher's summer workshop. The idea of summer homework is less than thrilling, but my teacher, Ms. Kartoffel, is the only teacher in school who is remotely awesome. I like to think I am her best student and that's why she offered me a free spot in her workshop. (I'll ignore the fact Manny Prince got into the workshop, too, because he draws about as well as a duckbill dipped in cow manure.)

And even if I wasn't at the workshop this summer, I could be hanging out with my friends. Rachel and Gwen are friends with Bertha and her sister Hilda Nguyen now, and they just had an inground swimming pool put in. And Penny Martinez-Snodgrass is working at the movie theater now. She'd be able to get us all in cheap!

My parents are in Tampa, Florida all summer. It seems like they're always away on business, but I guess they're not usually gone quite THIS long. That's why I'm being sent to my uncle's, as a type of familial babysitting.

Mom and Dad don't live a life of secrecy or action and adventure or anything like that. My dad is a small-time lawyer, though the hours don't reflect it, and my mom is an executive at a pharmaceutical company. Her work is opening a branch in Tampa where she's going to train new employees. Dad went along to keep her company, since he can work remotely. And they wanted to spend a few days of the summer on vacation.

I could have just gone to my aunt and uncle's place later in the summer, once my parents actually leave for their work/play date across the country. But, no. The idea this is a wonderful opportunity for me wormed itself into my parents' head: "Some time away from Irvine will be good for you!"

Well, no arguing with that, but I figured my "time away from Irvine" could have been "time spent at art camp."

Farewell, my Californian summer of art and bad horror movies. Hello, Washington.

Orcas Ferry

I've been on Orcas Island for about a week now. Uncle Pat's cabin is pretty spacious. I was kind of expecting a cave. It has three bedrooms, plus a small study off of the main living room. Almost everything in the cabin is made of wood, not like the particleboard homes around where I live. The door to my room is ***heavy***.

After getting the rundown of the cabin from Auntie, I trotted upstairs to unload some of my things in my new room for the summer. The bedroom was dark when I opened it, but since it was still daylight the room wasn't completely without shadows. I was able to maneuver my way through and dump my things onto my new, nicely made bed before I went back to find the light switch on the wall.

I was met with instant horror.

There, next to the light switch, was a framed painting. My hands twitched from wanting to tear it down and run for my life.

A clown. I HATE clowns. I hate clowns and sharks. Let that be known to the world. (I'm not overly fond of Miracle Whip either.)

This wasn't your garden-variety clown either. It was one of those weird jester clowns, wearing a bandit eye mask and face paint, decked out in tights and spangles.

Clowns of all sorts give me the creeps, but this one was looking malevolent and mischievous, the kind of clown whose jokes would be at my expense. Scribbled at the bottom, the name *Harlequin*.

My soul protested as I grabbed the frame off the wall, whimpering at having to touch it. I walked down the hall to Auntie's craft room and gingerly placed it in the desk.

But everything besides the psychopathic clown portrait hasn't been too bad.

Even if I did fall on our first hiking trip to Moran Park, I still got the chance to bring my sketchbook with me, which turned out to be a good thing since there were a couple elk in the area. I didn't even know what an elk looked like outside of pictures and TV, or that they were on Orcas Island.

It seemed like the entire island was lit up with blooming wildflowers. The different colors really stood out against all the green of the Pacific Northwest.

I thought there might be swarms of bugs, like the flies in summer back home. But it seemed like the majority were giant dragonflies and some small white butterflies fluttering in the forest flowers.

After the hike I had my first trip out to Fishing Bay in an attempt to see one of the local orca pods. We didn't see any, so I was a bit upset I didn't get to see the namesake of the island. (Okay, Uncle Pat told me Orcas Island wasn't named after orcas at all, but it was actually the shortened name of a Spaniard who came through the area. But I don't believe him.) It was still pretty fun, even without the whales. Seals were everywhere, and I even saw a few pups waiting for their moms to bring back a mouthful of salmon. And in the water there was a swarm of white moon jellyfish, from thumb-sized to bigger than my head.

(I did feel half-sick at first. I'm not used to small boats, and Auntie's tuna sandwiches didn't smell appetizing combined with the wharf aroma.)

On my third day here we went for a walk on the beach. I was thinking, **Oh. Beach. That means sand and bikinis**. I mean, summer is bikini season after all!

So shoot me. I didn't remember, unlike California, the beaches in Washington are completely muddy. The sand is like… not sand at all. It's just rocks instead. Slimy rocks, sticks, and seaweed, with evil little clams hiding below the mud. They can slice open your foot if you step wrong.

Auntie had the foresight to bring a sweatshirt for me, otherwise I'm pretty sure I'd have frozen to death. Even at the end of June, the weather next to the ocean inlet is chilly, with some pretty strong gusts from the air changing from spring to summer.

I'm starting to count the times where I've almost died or succumbed to injury from tripping over tree roots or slipping on algae-covered rocks... But it's hard to mind any of that when, overall, I've been having a good time. So far, anyway.

Usually I spend my summers sitting indoors where it's cooler, or at Rachel's house... where it's cooler. Or in the car... where it's cooler. Or going to 7-Eleven to get a slushie. (Can you guess why?) Here, I'm going out and doing things I wouldn't have had the chance to do at home. Seeing things I wouldn't have had the chance to see. The wildest animal I have ever seen at home is the raccoon that occasionally goes through our garbage.

Living in Irvine means that even though I'm technically close to the ocean, I don't go to it very often. Here, it's misty every morning, and sometimes I can smell the salty air of the ocean.

I love the trees, too. It's green year round in Washington. In Irvine you have to have a keen eye to notice any trees. And they're always trees the city has planted for "beautification." Little scraggly things, or palm trees. California cities are infested with palm trees. I love that here, there are hundred-foot fir trees. Everywhere.

There is a really… wild feel to everything. In some areas it's hard to imagine there are any humans living nearby at all. I don't think I remembered what clean air actually smelled like. Now when we get behind an old diesel truck I think, *Oh, that reminds me of home*.

I ran through an open patch of grass when we were hiking. The sensation of it between my toes made me feel like a little kid again. Of course, Uncle Pat would say, "You're still a little kid."

But, like all good things, it had to come to an end. Farewell, my days of fresh, clean grass, of butterflies, deer, and wildflowers.

Auntie said I should get a job. I asked why. She said, "Because it'd be good for you."

I said, "Nah. I'm good enough as it is."

Uncle Pat said, "No. Go get a job," and then launched into a rant about beach bum tourists, and having work ethics, and how as a kid he worked on a crab boat all summer long… Blah blah blah.

I mean, I've worked before. I was a Girl Scout for a year. And I've had to babysit a few times, so it's not like I'm completely inexperienced.

I guess when I get up tomorrow I'll go to Eastsound to hit up an internet cafe and check the newspaper. I can't understand why my relatives don't have a laptop. They're retired, and surely have enough money to afford one. Is the generation gap keeping them from making the leap into the digital age?

I knew I should have brought mine. The lack of internet is going to send me into withdrawals. I can sense it now.

I really don't want to get stuck in retail, but I guess everyone has to at some point. I'm hoping to find something more interesting, though. You know, unique.

Anyway, it's... uh... 11:30 now. I should go to sleep so I can get up early. Auntie and Uncle Pat always wake up at like, 5:00 a.m. Insane.

Good night, Journal.

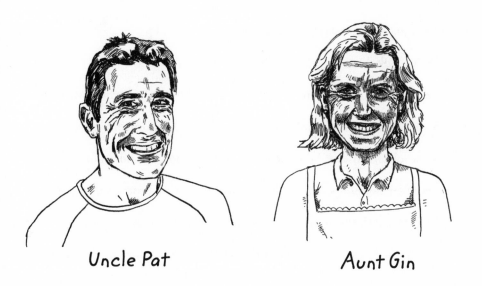

Uncle Pat   Aunt Gin

So, as I'm writing this, I'm sitting in a Starbucks, waiting for Uncle Pat to come by in his pickup truck to get me. They live far enough out of town—I can tell it's going to be a bit of a wait. I'd rather be in Auntie's car than Uncle Pat's pickup, but she's off setting up some sort of craft sale at a friend's.

The job market here seems about as lively as twice-over roadkill.

When I got up this morning, I thumbed through the paper, which was tiny for a Saturday issue. Tiny to me, anyway. I'm used to Californian papers. There were a few jobs listed, and I did the whole circling numbers and calling them thing in under two hours. They either wanted more work experience, or they had already filled the position. (Of course. Just my luck, right?)

So I suggested I get dropped off in Eastsound, thinking there might be an internet café nearby.

There wasn't.

But there was a fairly good-sized library that had computer access, so I popped on one of those for an hour. I went on all the job lists sites and I even checked Orcas Island's main city/island website to see if they had anything available for young adults, like maybe working at a summer camp.

I called and called from my cell phone, thankful I didn't have to pay to use any of the library's landlines. Then I emailed, then took a break for lunch, and then called some more.

It sounded like the only thing available for just the summer, for someone with next to no "valid" work experience, was a job swabbing off yachts at the marina down at Judd Bay. They even mentioned something about me maybe having to chip off barnacles. Not particularly thrilling.

I called and told Auntie and Uncle Pat they wanted me to interview. I was hoping they would take pity on my soul and say it was fine to NOT work for the rest of the summer, but no. Uncle Pat sounded happy on the phone, like we were two peas in a pod getting stuck with horrible jobs as youths.

So I resigned myself to my fate and made my way to Starbucks, where Pat is going to pick me up. It would have made my life a lot easier if I had my laptop—I could have simply used the wireless connection in Starbucks. But I figured it was too bulky to pack, so I'm left with nothing but public desktops.

On the walk to Starbucks I noticed a pop can lying on the sidewalk, with a bin just a few feet away down an old, dirty alley.

It was gross, you know? I've started to really like the San Juans, and I saw this can and figured I'd toss it. So I trotted down the alley like a good citizen and threw the can into the proper bin.

Then this flier that was tacked up on a wooden retaining board caught my eye.

I can't even begin to wonder why someone put a flier there. There's no way anyone would see it—it was obvious no one went down that alley very frequently. And, on top of that, it was a completely hideous flier—all sepia and in a completely boring font. It looked old, like it had been through a few rainstorms. I was ready to rip it off the wall and throw it away, but luckily I read the flier before deciding to dunk it into the trash bin like a make-believe basketball star.

It read, and I quote:

Natural History Illustrator Wanted.
No experience necessary.
Must have fine artistic skill.

And the date was recent! I mean, it sounded weird, but it would sure as hell beat washing down rich folks' boats all summer.

I called the number and this old guy answered. He sounded no-nonsense like my uncle, but a bit odd, too. He asked the basics: How old I was, where I was from… and then gave me the address for my interview.

I was pretty stoked, but cautious. I had some time before Uncle Pat was supposed to pick me up, so I ran back to the library to look at a map and see where the house was. And to make sure the house didn't belong to, like, a sexual predator or something.

So I called Uncle Pat back and told him about it. I don't know if he was happy I got an interview or mad I didn't end up with a job scraping scabs off of burn victims or whatever he considered real work.

I see him pulling up outside, so I better go.

Bye for now, Journal.

Okay, Journal. I'm just going to jump right in here.

That was the WEIRDEST experience of my entire life. I have this foreboding feeling it's going to get stranger from here on out. So maybe I should tack on a "so far."

I'm back at the cabin now, but this day couldn't get any stranger if it tried.

I didn't bring any professional-looking clothes with me, since I didn't expect to be working while here on, you know, *vacation*, so I asked Auntie if she had anything I could wear. For what I had to work with, I thought I looked pretty good. (Definitely not comfortable, though. When I got home I immediately switched to bumming-around-the-house/cabin pajamas.)

The interview was at 4:30. Uncle Pat drove me and stuck around outside in his truck to make sure I was safe.

The house was… well, it was like one of those old houses you only see in horror movies. It was near the water and the paint was chipping off the siding. It looked like a strong wind could just—push—and it'd come crumbling down.

But it was certainly a pretty area, I'll give it that much.

An old guy met me at the door. He was Orville Tanner, the guy on the phone yesterday. His hair is gray… I would guess he's around 65 or so.

If I mysteriously end up missing and all that's left of me is this journal, go arrest that guy.

Mr. Tanner's House

Inside the house… Oh lord, inside the house. Where to even begin?

There were two long halls off to each side. The entryway itself was high and narrow, with a chandelier hanging in the open area above.

I've been in old houses before, but this one was even stranger than old Miss Battler's house. And she has individual rooms for her ferrets.

Mr. Tanner told me to follow him. We went down the left hall. I noticed photos lining the walls. Not just any photos, though. Old photography. And illustrations. You know, the kind people made on their first expeditions into the West.

By the time we reached his office we had passed a bunch of closed doors. I was nearly certain I was in a psychopath's house. I was kind of expecting ominous music to start playing, even more so when we entered his office. He had me sit down in this big, cushy, old leather chair and excused himself.

There were jars full of things I didn't even want to know about, and what appeared to be the complete skeleton of some weird sea creature hanging above the desk. He had a fossilized elephant tusk hanging on the wall. I think it was an elephant tusk, anyway. Now that I think about it, it looked pretty similar to the mammoth tusk I saw at the Page Museum... I think I probably jumped half a foot when he came back, since I was so preoccupied looking around the room.

I barely remember any of the interview itself, I was so nervous. I know I gave him my sketchbook to flip through, and I remember how his face kind of twisted as he looked at it.

I sweat more than I had hiking last week, partially from stress and partially from it being, like, 90 degrees in there.

Are all job interviews like that? Because if so, I am really not looking forward to the future.

Mammoth Tus

Creatures of unknown origin inside those jars were looking at me. I kept picturing what would happen if one of them moved: Me, running out of the house, screaming like a five year old.

Nightmares. I'm going to have nightmares tonight.

But anyway, almost 45 minutes later... (I, by the way, have no fingernails left) he actually hired me!

I'm still shocked, truth be told. I want to say it seems too good to be true, but my mind keeps replaying everything that happened... the smells and the creepy doll eyes of the pickled specimens and the death grins of the skeletons and skulls...

I was kind of having second thoughts as we went over salary and hours. But then his son or nephew popped in with some tea...

I didn't catch his name, but let's just say I may be slightly more eager to work there until the break is over.

This will be an interesting summer.

Ugh. My hair still smells musty from that house. It reminds me of that time I came out of my friend Jessie's house smelling like cigarette smoke from her dad's den. (Not that horrible, of course. This smells like books, dust, and old guy rather than cigarettes, cigars, and old guy.)

Anyway, I'm going to go help Auntie with dinner sooo…

Good night, Journal.

Mr. Tanner

Sorry I haven't written in you for a few days, Journal.

Man, last week was awesome. Have you ever seen fireworks light up an entire island? Or reflect on the sea at night?

It's amazingly beautiful.

I could see fireworks from all the nearby islands: San Juan, Lummi, Lopez, Shaw, and Sucia were some Uncle Pat pointed out to me. Off in the distance I could see a few from Fidalgo and Whidbey Islands as well.

Uncle Pat told me the reservations made it really easy for everyone in Washington to get big fireworks, even though it wasn't technically legal to bring them off of the reservations. Everyone on Orcas seemed to go to Lummi Island, or to the mainland to the Tulalip tribe to get theirs.

Unfortunately, Uncle Pat was a bit… well, Auntie used the word "hardheaded" about the issue. We bought only the state-allowed fireworks (which were sparklers and land-bound little things), while everyone else had giant, colorful displays that went up into the air. At least we could still see them all around, even if we couldn't set off our own.

The smell of powder in the air was strong enough I could smell it on my hair later.

So in my last entry I told you how I got the job, right? That was on the third, and obviously there wasn't going to be any working on the Fourth of July.

Mr. Tanner told me to come in the next Monday, the 11th, which, as you can tell, is today.

Auntie could tell I was nervous before my first day, so for the rest of the week we just kicked back in the sun, and walked around some of the island. It was a beautiful July week. The weather was just right. I even got a bit of a tan. I didn't think it was possible for a California gal to get a tan in Washington. I mean, it is the land of rain and overcast weather.

Anyway I know this is short, but I have to go to work now. So nervous.

5:20 p.m.

Okay. Where to even start...

When I arrived, Mr. Tanner directed me down to the dock by their old, weird, probably haunted house. Behind the house, the dock wrapped down from a sizable porch to the beach.

I was just happy I didn't have to go into the house again. For the time being.

Anyway, Mr. Tanner told me I'd be drawing specimens. Mr. Tanner's grandson, Charles, gave me a fold out chair and I sat myself up down by the muck. (Well, Mr. Tanner called him Charles. He whispered to me, "Just call me Charlie.")

I had a new sketchbook, a case of good pencils, and a special waterproof notebook for notes and grafts for plotting areas of the island we'd be working in. I felt very professional.

Until Charlie handed me a very large bucket full of mud and murky water.

"Go ahead. Dig in," he told me, straight-faced.

Dig in? Do you know WHAT I had to pull out of the soil and silt?

A geoduck.

Do you know what a geoduck looks like? No? Consider yourself very, very lucky.

Charlie said some people eat these things. Raw, like mollusc sushi. They're even pronounced weird. It's not "geo-duck," it's "gooey-duck." Gooey duck! I mean, really! I suppose they had to give a weird thing a weird name to complete the cycle of insanity.

I dropped the creature onto the ground. From the porch, Mr. Tanner bit out a comment about me being more careful with the specimens.

The face I made when picking up the creature again must have amused Charlie. Even his grandfather seemed to have one of those all-knowing smirks on his face. You know, the really aggravating kind.

I laid the gargantuan mollusc out on a white tarp on the ground, with a bed of water and mud around it since it's accustomed to a wet, murky life.

Charlie was rattling off facts faster than I could keep up. I stopped once when he told me how large the stupid thing's "foot" could get. Up to three feet. Yuck.

After about a half hour, Charlie and Mr. Tanner said they were going inside to take care of a few things, which left me to my lonesome on the beach, on a rickety fold out chair with my drawing book and a mollusc that looked vaguely obscene.

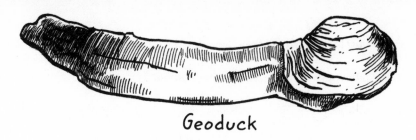

Geoduck

It was around 8:30 a.m. and the sun hadn't really come out. I was getting quite cold, and I was starting to hyper-focus on the smell of stale sea air. I heard seabirds and seals nearby making a ruckus.

I was glaring at the geoduck the entire time I was drawing it, like it had personally offended me. Maybe it made a crack about my mother or something. Either way.

Eliza was not a happy camper.

I must have looked as miserable as I felt amongst the geoducks. And trust me, I was miserable. Little thunderbolts were shooting out of my own personal little rolling, roaring storm system above my head.

By 9:45 the winds right off the sound had picked up. I was very cold, and growing more and more uncomfortable on the stupid little hard-as-a-plank fold out chair. And that damn geoduck just sat there on the tarp. Like it knew. Like it was taunting my every move.

By 10:00 I had a few drawings and a sketch of the geoduck finished. Charlie came out and trotted off down the coastline, holding a bucket and a pair of rubber gloves. I played with the idea of pitching the mollusc at his head.

A few minutes later, Mr. Tanner came down to the beach. He peered at my drawings, glancing between them and the geoduck.

That was nerve-wracking. I mean, this was my first day on the job, and I wasn't even halfway through the day. What if he rethought hiring me after seeing my field drawings?

Thankfully, he just nodded and made a low humming noise. I hoped that meant, "Good job, Eliza. Here is an interesting specimen for you to draw. Come to the porch and have a cup of hot tea."

I was very, very wrong.

Charlie came back, dirty and muddy. And with a full bucket. He dumped it out. It had three more geoducks in it. All three, thankfully, smaller and slightly less grotesque than the one I had been drawing.

But the point still stands. Four geoducks in one day.

Mr. Tanner told me to work on drawing them until noon, then I'd have a lunch break before getting back to work. I'm certain he believed himself kind when he told me he'd let me off work at 4:00 rather than 5:00.

Charlie bid me adieu, almost containing his amusement, and I was left alone. Again. In the cold. On a piece of what was certainly the most uncomfortable material to sit on. With three geoducks. On a tarp. In seawater, mud, and muck.

And that's where I was until lunch. After a tuna sandwich and an orange, I worked in the same place until I had to go home.

Geoducks

The second I walked in the door, Auntie cheered, "Congratulations on your first day of work!"

Uncle Pat gave me a hearty thump on the back and I almost fell flat on my face. Auntie must have noticed I looked like warmed-over death, because she said my congratulatory dinner could wait and I should take a shower to freshen up. I asked her if we could have a clam bake. I was thinking of eating the geoducks' distant relatives out of spite.

So, after a good, long soak, I'm here in my room. The smell of food is drifting up the wooden stairs, and after a relatively small lunch it smells really good.

I think I may go partake in the festivities.

Do you think Uncle Pat would be *too* upset if I told him I wanted to quit one day into my first job? I don't know if I can deal with more elephant-like molluscs.

Before I completely kill my appetite thinking about geoducks, I think I'll go eat.

Good night, Journal.

DER...

July 12 — 8:14 p.m.

Last night I told Uncle Pat and Auntie I wanted to quit. It was miserable work, and I was tired and completely run-down after only one day.

Auntie seemed understanding enough. She had seen how gaunt and pale my face was after the first day. Uncle Pat was… less so.

He was upset. He didn't think it was right to quit so quickly. He said I should stick with things till the end because of the "promises" I made. I had entered into an agreement with the Tanners, myself, and my family.

I was feeling kind of guilty until he started talking about how my parents didn't raise me right. How his brother, my dad, had failed, and how my folks weren't tough enough on me.

Not tough enough on me? Yeah, maybe. It's kind of hard to be tough on your kids if you're barely even there. I thought he understood that. I thought maybe he was offering to house me for the summer because he knew I'd be entirely alone in California.

The next part didn't go so well. I admit, I talked back a little. So he started yelling. He said I was as bad as my father, worse even, and he had been proud, and I crushed it.

By the end I was yelling, too. Dinner was ruined. I felt so bad for Auntie— she didn't know how to react. I was going to come back downstairs after the fight to help her clean up, but I couldn't stand the thought of running into Pat, so I fumed in my room all night. I barely got any sleep, even though I was so tired I could barely keep my eyes open.

I was up and out of the house by 6:30 a.m., barely acknowledging Pat, who just shot me a look. Thankfully, Auntie was enough on my side she was willing to give me a ride to work.

He thought I wouldn't see anything through till the end? Yeah, well, he could watch me stick with my plan of quitting.

When I got to the Tanner house I rapped on the door, harder than I would have otherwise. I was pissed and the whole world needed to know.

In the back of my mind I remembered Uncle Pat sitting in his truck to make sure I was safe during my interview.

Charlie answered. He had a bright smile and a glint in his eyes. "Come on in. I want to show you something, Eliza."

Suddenly I didn't feel angry anymore. I just felt tired. So very tired. But I still knew I needed to quit. I followed Charlie inside, thinking it'd be easier to tell him instead of his grandfather.

I wasn't very thrilled with the idea of going into their weird house again, but I wasn't thinking much at the time. I couldn't bring myself to think about much more than how nice and shiny Charlie's hair looked from the back.

This time, I was led down the right-hand hallway. We passed more shut doors, much like the first time I was here. There were still pictures lining the hallway. I spotted a few of what I thought might be a little Charlie, but the pictures seemed too old to be him. Maybe his grandfather as a child. Or great-grandfather even.

We turned a corner and he led me into a small room. It was friendlier than the room I was in for the interview. The walls had an old-fashioned wallpaper and the rug was deep red. There were little cubbies along the walls. Some had packages and papers in them. In the middle of the room there was a round, wooden table where something large laid, covered by a cream-colored cloth.

"This," Charlie said, "is what you'll be drawing today."

He pulled back the cloth to reveal a giant cow skull. He told me it was a *Bison antiquus.*

It was big—bigger than bison today, which is saying something. I have a distant memory of a bison charging our car at a nature park when I was a little kid. This skull's horn points were at least three feet across from tip to tip, if not bigger. It was an impressive sight, to say the least.

Charlie told me another *Bison antiquus* was found in an Orcas Island peat bog not too long ago, and the demand for more skeletal remains was high. He told me this specimen was around 16,000 years old, older the other found on Orcas Island, but still well within the realm of normal since the *Bison antiquus* lived on the island as far back as 18,000 years ago.

I asked if either skeleton had been hunted by the native peoples, remembering Charlie said the Nisqually tribe lived in this area for thousands of years, and the word *geoduck* was derived from their language.

He said neither specimen had been hunted. They died of natural causes, most likely disease.

When I asked how he could possibly know how it died, he just smiled and told me he had developed a sense for things like that over the years. I imagine having Mr. Tanner as his grandfather must have given him a weirdly encyclopedic knowledge of ancient dead species. I'm sure this is a useful skill in some circles.

He asked me if I wanted to start drawing.

I hesitated. I wasn't sure what to do. I went there to quit.

I asked Charlie if I could have a drink while I worked. He smiled, and a few minutes later I had a steaming cup of Earl Grey tea in one hand and a pencil in the other. This time I had a comfortable padded chair to sit in, and Charlie stayed in the room to talk with me.

While I drew he told me things about the ancient bison's life. How their ancestors, *Bison priscus*, came from Siberia and crossed into Alaska. How a number of species like the long-horned bison, *Bison latifrons*, came and went, leading up to the success of the *Bison antiquus*. While the majority died off when most megafauna did (around 10,000 years ago), at their peak their range stretched from parts of Western and Central Canada, down the West Coast, and into Mexico.

Bison antiquus was far more prevalent than his cousin *latifrons*, and most likely inhabited open woodlands and savannah rather than heavily wooded areas like *Bison latifrons* probably had. *Bison antiquus'* remains were commonly found in La Brea Tar Pits, Charlie added, knowing I must be partial to things in my own state.

I didn't even realize how much time had passed until Charlie said it was past 1:00, and how sorry he was he'd made me miss my lunch. I didn't really mind, though.

We sat on the back porch and watched the water while we ate. Sitting by the waterfront yesterday seemed almost like years ago.

After about fifteen minutes, he clapped me on the back and pointed to something out in the water.

An orca pod.

Charlie said the Tanner family picked this spot on Orcas Island years and years ago because it was so full of wildlife, and the first day they arrived they saw an orca pod right about where we were looking.

For something called a killer whale, they seemed so graceful. But I suppose that's the way predators are. Felines and canines are well known for their graceful hunting approaches.

When we went back to the room with the *Bison antiquus* skull, time passed just as quickly as it had before. Before I knew it, Mr. Tanner popped his head into the room, told me it was 6:00, and he didn't pay overtime.

I was there from 7:00 a.m. to 6:00 p.m. and never realized. I was so caught up talking with Charlie I lost track of time. As someone who usually watches the clock tick down the seconds in school, this was odd for me.

Charlie gave me a ride home. When I got here, Auntie greeted me nervously. Uncle Pat was sitting in the kitchen. He didn't look thrilled, and I figured Auntie must have talked to him while I was at work. I should have known that wouldn't help much—Walcotts are known for being stubborn as mules. I wondered if he brooded all day, or if he went to pout with some of his buddies on the island.

Auntie asked how it went, if I had quit. She asked why I was gone so long. I told her now I have no intentions of quitting. She hugged me, and when we sat down to dinner I saw Uncle Pat smiling faintly.

I said to him, "I didn't not quit because of anything you said. I went there to quit, but I made up my own mind from there on."

Dinner was quiet, and not exactly relaxing, until I told Auntie I saw orcas. Uncle Pat gruffly asked which pod it was.

Anyway, I'm in my room again, after a very long day. I'm tired, but I don't know... happy, I guess? Things don't seem as horrible as they did last night. I might cut someone if I have to draw another geoduck again, though.

Bison antiquus skull

Mr. Tanner said tomorrow would be a big day, and when I looked to Charlie he just smiled and said, "Don't worry. No mud."

It'd be nice if we could go into town, maybe see people closer to our age. I'm not sure if he has any friends here or not. There's a pretty big absence of teenagers on Orcas, besides a few on vacation, so who knows.

I miss my friends.

I'm going to try and get a good night's sleep. It's only 8:50, but I figure I'll probably need energy for tomorrow.

Good night, Journal.

Charlie called a few minutes ago. Apparently, I'm going to meet him and Mr. Tanner at the local lime quarry. I wasn't even aware there was a lime quarry on Orcas Island.

Thankfully, Auntie knew where it was. I asked her for a ride, since I'm still not entirely comfortable asking Uncle Pat. I can't even begin to imagine how unbearably awkward that car ride would be.

Anyway, I figure quarries are bound to be dirty, so I'm wearing some of my ugliest clothes. I hope Charlie doesn't think I look like a crazy woman who throws cats at people.

I might as well put my hair back, too. It's gotten in the way a few times because of the wind. Kind of hard to concentrate on drawing specific features when you're spitting hair out of your mouth every five seconds.

I gotta go, but I'll pack you along with me. Might get a chance to write more during lunch.

12:35 p.m.

Charlie is staring at me right now.

Oh, yes, **Chuck**. I am writing about you. In my journal. And you shall never see. Keep looking. Unless you have super powers you will never know what I'm saying about you.

You deserve this for trying to steal my apple.

Anyway. I'm on my lunch break, if you couldn't tell. We're lounging around on some of the bigger rocks in the quarry.

When I got here Charlie told me we'd be looking for Devonian brachiopods. I had heard of the word *brachiopod* before, but I wasn't sure what they were. And I knew even less about the Devonian period. When I asked, I was given Charlie's encyclopedic knowledge of them both in five seconds.

Mr. Tanner said, "Charles, stop showing off."

Which is just insane. He wasn't showing off for me—never mind. It doesn't matter anyway.

The lime quarry here is full of brachiopods from the middle of the Devonian era. What are these amazing things, you may ask?

Fossil-wise, they look similar to many molluscs, but they are not molluscs at all. There are still some alive today, but the ones we've been hunting are most assuredly dead and gone. The Devonian period lasted from… I think they said around 416 million years ago to roughly 359 million years ago. Charlie added it was during the Devonian that lobe-finned fish first evolved pelvic bones and the beginnings of legs.

To be honest, finding one of those fish, one of the first steps in the evolutionary chain, would be far more fascinating than finding one of these brachiopods. There are tons of them! I have a sneaking suspicion I'm going to end up drawing them, too. Mr. Tanner keeps organizing them on a plot by species and year.

I'm actually beginning to recognize some of the scientific names being rattled off at me. At one point today, when Charlie handed me a type of Spiriferida, I nodded and put it in the right time plot. I thought he was going to hug me. It must be lonely being the only teenager on the planet who knows the difference between a Devonian Lingulata brachiopod and a Late Cretaceous Rhynchonellida brachiopod.

Anyway, lunch is over. I better get back to work. Apparently I'm going to be drawing a jillion little fossils. Gee, what fun.

I'll write more later.

5:20 p.m.

I have a hand cramp. I didn't know you could get hand cramps.

Since lunch, I've drawn more brachiopods than I can even begin to count. There were at least... 250, if not more. I drew every single one we dug up, organized by time frame and size. The time frames were Early Devonian, Middle Devonian, and Late Devonian. Since we were working with over a million years difference between Early and Late, it wasn't easy to plot them, but we did it as accurately as possible.

Mr. Tanner was amazing. He could see different colors in the soil and lime and be able to judge a time frame by it. I mean, he could have been completely making it up and I wouldn't know the difference, but I trust him. He seems like the type of person who takes his work very seriously.

Mr. Tanner said my drawings would be a good resource to look back on while they continue their research around the quarry, and would give good insight into the environment at the time. Like, a bunch of adult fossils would indicate a time of prosperity and lack of predators, but a bunch of young fossils in bad condition might indicate a more turbulent life.

We didn't find too many young ones. Most species of the time must have flourished—well, except the Pentamerida… Mr. Tanner said they didn't survive much longer than the Devonian.

It's odd to think out of the 5,000 genera of the past, there are only around 100 living today. That aspect of it was pretty interesting, but I could have gone without drawing THAT many in one sitting.

Thankfully, my experience drawing those damn geoducks proved useful in drawing the brachiopods, though I'd never admit that to Mr. Tanner or Charlie.

Anyway, Auntie's here to get me (finally), so I gotta go. I'm starving, so I'm going to go eat more than I should and then soak in the clawfoot tub for an hour.

Bye for now, Journal.

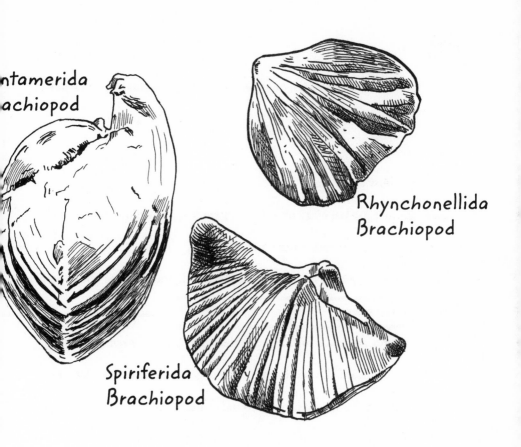

ntamerida
achiopod

Rhynchonellida
Brachiopod

Spiriferida
Brachiopod

Okay, I know I haven't written anything in the last few days, but I've been busy!

Sort of busy.

Okay, not busy at all, really.

Let's see, since my last entry on the 13th I worked a few more days at the lime quarry, continuing our work on the brachiopod deposits. On Friday, as we were packing up our equipment and bags of books, Mr. Tanner told me not to bother showing up next week.

I had a mild heart attack for a minute, thinking, ***But I've been working so hard lately!*** Charlie quickly cut in with, "We're going away for a week or so… hopefully, anyway. We should be back Monday after next." I was curious.

Mr. Tanner said they would be on an "expedition." I didn't ask him to explain. It seemed like he wouldn't have told me anyway, and Charlie was making a just-don't-ask face.

I'd think they were secret agents, but I highly doubt there are such boring secret agents as these two, digging around in mud and quarries in hopes of finding fossils or other historical remnants.

Charlie

Sure, I might miss sitting around at lunch, chewing on one of Auntie's homemade sandwiches, listening to them talk about the things they've found in the past. But I was looking forward to having a week to myself, too.

Before I could start dreaming of a week filled with shaved ice, grilled food, and island exploring, Mr. Tanner assigned me work to do while they were gone.

I have to draw a re-creation of some of the habitats from the Eocene, based on things found in the Chuckanut formation, a geologic formation that runs through a good portion of Washington. (You are allowed to laugh at the name "Chuckanut" as long as you aren't around Mr. Tanner.) Given my complete lack of knowledge of either subject, a library visit was necessary.

My drawings aren't finished yet, and the week is almost up so I'm a little worried. But I have the weekend to finish them, and it's not like Mr. Tanner will know I waited until the last minute.

I'm trying to keep as true to the time period as possible, and it's difficult. At one point I yelled, "Who cares about ancient softshell turtles?!" in the library.

The Eocene lasted from roughly 56 to 34 million years ago. The Chuckanut formation contains remnants of plants and animal life from most of the epoch. It's a long time, and you can't put something from the Lutetian Eocene in the habitat of something from the Priabonian Eocene, unless the species did happen to live that long in the same general area.

The most important thing about re-creating the habitat is looking at the fossilized plant life—at least for me, anyway. It gives me a good idea of how plentiful plant life was, along with the temperament of the climate in the area at the time.

As far as I can tell, the Eocene was primarily a subtropical climate. There are fossilized plant records of everything from tree ferns to swamp cypress trees. Again, these are over 34 million years old. There is evidence of ancient palm trees, too, and I have to wonder if they'd look much like the palm trees around my house in California.

There's not much evidence of animal fossils, but animal tracks aren't uncommon. The Chuckanut formation seemed to be a coastal environment at the time, when water levels were higher. The books I was reading covered the types of mammalian, bird, and reptile life that lived in these places.

As much as I've been involved in my research here I keep thinking about the Tanners.

On Monday, I asked Auntie why they didn't tell me where they were going. She shrugged, but Uncle Pat said something about how archaeologists in South America had been killed by grave and treasure robbers. Maybe the Tanners were facing a similar threat and didn't want to get me involved.

I wanted to say something biting back to him, but the more I thought about it the more it sounded plausible. Until he said maybe *they* were the grave robbers.

I didn't yell, but I said I knew them better than he did, and they would never do something like that.

Eocene Chuckanut

But now that I think about it, I don't really know them that well... And they did have that *Bison antiquus* skull... The first one found on Orcas Island had been a shock to the scientific public, yet it didn't seem like anyone knew about this one. Is it possible they managed to find it without anyone finding out?

Where could they possibly be? They brought me along on their trip to the lime quarry. Is it farther than that? So far they'd be gone for a whole week? What are they doing that's so secretive they can't tell me? I know I've only been working with them for a short period, but I think Charlie trusts me... at least a little.

I'm sure they had legal access to the lime quarry, but now I'm starting to question everything and anything Tanner related...

Why on Earth do they need me to draw their findings? Why not take pictures? It would be much easier that way. Is Mr. Tanner just a traditionalist? Or is there a reason they don't want any photographic evidence?

What if I'm aiding criminals?

It's Monday evening. This morning I went to the Tanners' house. (I'd say bright

and early, but it was so overcast and misty out.) I knocked on the front door.

I didn't see any cars in the driveway, besides Auntie who was waiting for me. I

told her I'd give her the high sign to go if someone was home, or I'd get back in

the car if I didn't see anyone after a few minutes.

None of the house lights were on. I was about to leave, but on a whim I

circled back behind the house to the porch.

There was fog rolling off the tops of the breaking waves. It was difficult to see,

but in the distance I saw a dark shadow bobbing towards me. For a moment I

wanted to hightail it out of there, screaming NESSIE! But as the shadow came

closer I could tell it was a boat. There were people on it, and they were cloaked

in shadow. I remembered my paranoid suspicions.

As the figures became clearer I could tell it was Mr. Tanner and Charlie.

Charlie was waving from the bow and Mr. Tanner was steering the boat. It

wasn't a huge boat, but it was big enough to carry something large and wrapped

in white.

I waved and made the one-minute gesture before darting back around front.

I told Auntie they were back and she could go home, and I'd call her on my cell

when I needed to be picked up again.

When I returned to the dock, the Tanners were just pulling up. Charlie hopped over the side and tied up the boat.

He looked a bit… well, like he had been camping for a week and had no access to showers or washing machines. His clothes were messed up and dirty, and it looked like he had been splashed by a few waves. His dark hair was unusually dirty and limp, and his blue eyes were worn and tired.

I offered to help. He shook it off and said I could help him inside after they moved the specimen.

The specimen.

Mr. Tanner moved himself out of the boat and said I should be grateful to get the chance to work on something like this. Charlie and Mr. Tanner carefully lifted up the large specimen with a makeshift pulley system. They maneuvered it onto a cart—quite the feat, given its size.

I felt kind of stupid watching them work, but I didn't want to overstep my boundaries. I followed them silently as they went into the house through the back door, a way I wasn't familiar with. There was a large, open green house-like room with lots of different plants I had never seen before.

We left that room quickly and passed into a small, wide hallway with very old statues standing guard at either side. I followed them into a small room that looked like a chef's kitchen, with cold, hard floors and metallic sinks and appliances.

Before I could get a good eyeful, we entered a large area that looked like a science classroom. There were desks and instruments lying around, with sinks in the far back, along with glass cabinets full of creatures. I was instantly reminded of being back in Mr. Tanner's study for my interview—with the whale skeleton and things in jars.

I heard the weight of linens fall to the ground.

I turned around to see a huge skull. The skull of what, I didn't know. But whatever it was, it was amazing. And terrifying. There were so many sharp teeth, it looked like it could easily tear something else in two.

"This is *Maiacetus inuus*," Charlie announced. He looked pleased with himself. He continued with, "It's one of the stages land mammals took to becoming sea life again."

My guess would have been a dinosaur of some sort, so I was glad I didn't say anything.

"Eocene?" I asked, wondering if this was part of the reason I had been drawing Eocene habitats from the Chuckanut formation.

I received nods of confirmation, and then Mr. Tanner said, "I want you to draw it. If you could finish it by the end of today, that would be good. Charles and I will be back shortly."

Charlie pulled a book from a cabinet, flipped to the appropriate section, handed it to me, and then followed his grandfather out. I was left alone with the skull. I looked down at the book and read about *Maiacetus*, its life in the ocean, and the possibility of it being amphibious, given its small back legs yet otherwise sea-life-like appearance.

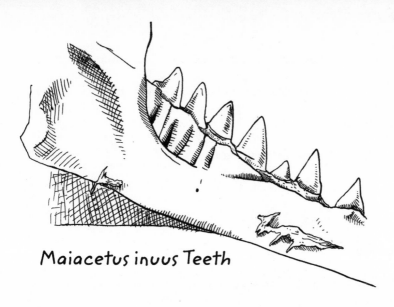

Maiacetus inuus Teeth

I settled down in a chair next to the skull and pulled out my drawing supplies. I drew for a few moments before I noticed something weird.

This was not a fossil. It was a long-dead creature that should have been fossilized, but it was NOT a fossil. It was just a skeleton.

I leaned in closer. My heart raced when I saw it.

Tissue. As in flesh tissue. Muscle tissue. On something that's been dead for nearly 47 million years. Right there, on the jawline… near those giant teeth.

Just then Charlie and Mr. Tanner came back, looking clean and upbeat… well, at least Charlie looked upbeat.

I was so freaked out I didn't say much. I tried to focus on what was in front of me.

For the rest of the day I worked in a daze. I'm still in a daze. I don't know what to do. Something weird is going on. Maybe something weird was always going on… the job poster… the house that's more like a maze than a home… it's more a home to skeletons and fossils than actual humans.

I'm going to go back to the house. I just need to check a few things. (Never underestimate a California girl's ability to snoop.)

I'll write more when I get home… provided I get home and I'm not abducted by aliens or something.

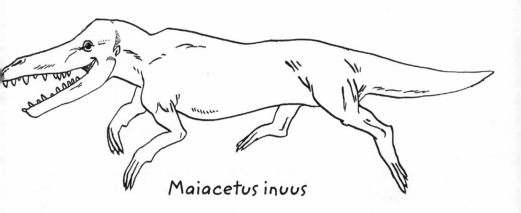

Maiacetus inuus

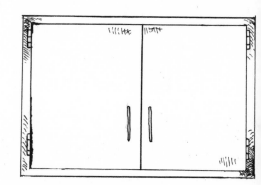

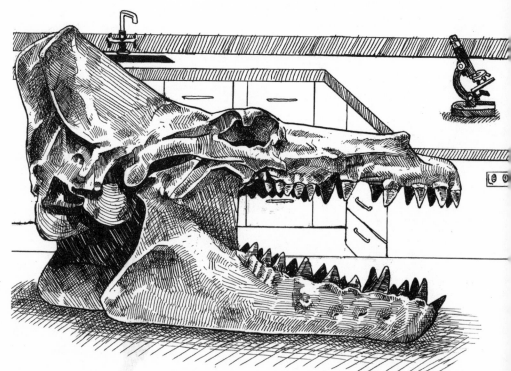

Maiacetus innus Skull

July 26 (barely) 5:10 a.m.

I *haven't slept yet.* There are a lot of things I need to say, and I need to say them all in about five minutes so I can take a nap before going back to work.

If I go back to work at all.

Okay. Where to start.

I waited till just after 1:00 a.m. to sneak out of the house. I took Auntie's car—not something I'm particularly proud of. I can drive fine, but I don't exactly have a real license yet, just a learner's permit. But she did say I could take the car in an emergency. This might not have exactly counted as an emergency, but I don't think she'll mind. Or even notice, since the gas gauge hardly moved at all.

I took the car out to the Tanners' house. I parked down the road a bit so no one would hear me driving up. I was decked out in blacks and grays, with my hair tucked up into a stocking cap. I figured my light hair might be more visible, and I didn't want to chance anything. Or maybe I just wanted to look like a secret agent/ ninja.

Thankfully, the first week I was here I got a pair of boots. They came in handy on the beach and out in the lime quarry, where my sandals just wouldn't have cut it. They also made skulking up to the Tanner house easier, as I was able to brush through the grass and weeds rather quickly.

I avoided walking along the porch and deck, though, fearing the boots would make too much noise on the wooden posts. I opted to round the other side of the house, the same side as Mr. Tanner's study. There was no porch, and it was up against woods, which made staying hidden way easier, even though I flinched and froze every time I crunched on leaves or twigs.

I made it up to a window on the ground level. I couldn't see anything at first. All the lights were off. It looked like Orville and Charles Tanner had gone to bed.

But then I noticed a weird reddish light coming from the corner. I tried to get a better look, but it was farther down the hallway at an angle I couldn't see very well from my snooping spot outside the window.

I noticed another window a few feet down. I carefully crouched and moved, again having mini-heart attacks every single time my boots crushed a small branch. This window was a little higher than the other one, and I had to stand on my tippy toes to see in. I could see the light leaking through, just faintly lighting up the branches of the evergreen trees. But before I could see anything, something solid bumped into my right leg and I fell backwards. I gasped, but thankfully I didn't yelp or scream.

I looked to my right to see what had hit me, my heart racing about 800 beats a minute. I froze. My blood ran cold.

It was a full-grown raccoon, the size of a Cocker Spaniel. It may not have been very threatening if I'd been standing up, but I was on my ass—and almost eye to eye with it. I'd heard of people's dogs and cats being killed by raccoons, and here I was six inches away from one's fangs. I was pretty sure death by raccoon would be the stupidest death ever. But the fuzzy, banded beast looked up at the window I was peeking in.

The red light switched to a sickly, acid green. The raccoon puffed out and bolted into the forest, and another crawled out from under the house and followed him. I didn't blame them. I felt afraid, like I should have been running away too.

I was shaking. I stood up slowly and tried to get another look in the window.

A bilious green light was seeping out from under a closed door. It wasn't Mr. Tanner's study, but another room I must have passed on the way to it. I could tell there were shadows moving underneath the door. I figured it had to be Mr. Tanner and Charlie. It looked like only two people.

Soon the green light began to flicker, and out poured an even brighter beam of indigo light. This pulsed alternately with the same red light I saw at first. It was certainly strange, but I couldn't see anything in the way of damning evidence. Just weird lights.

Until this happened:

It was a bright light, brighter than any of the others. For a few milliseconds (though it felt like forever), it appeared to be day again. And then the scent of green grass and wildflowers washed over me like a wave.

The light died and I saw spots in my vision. My mind reeled in attempts to explain the smell that was certainly not the crisp smell of the forest around me.

One more light pulsed, only once. It was orange, a bright neon orange with a tinge of red.

I felt like I was going to be violently ill. My entire body shook. My head started to spin and I decided it was time to get the hell out of there. As quietly as I could, I rounded the house and snuck down the road to Auntie's car. I stumbled a few times—I was still dizzy, and the spots in my sight didn't help with night vision, but I made it there in one piece. As far as I could tell, no one noticed me.

The farther I moved from the house, the less horrible I felt, and by the time I got back to the cabin I didn't feel awful at all. That didn't keep my knees and hands from shaking—they're still shaking. I changed out of my snooping clothes and I'm just... sitting on the bed for a while.

I feel like I'm trying to digest a whole bunch of facts, but I didn't really learn anything (besides the Tanners have a magical orange light that makes people want to crawl in a hole and die).

They could have just been watching TV. Right? Right. Maybe the flashing lights just… shocked my senses. After being outside in the dark, they were just too much for my system to handle. That makes sense.

Yeah. Right.

This is going to make work insanely awkward. I think I'll ask Auntie not to make me tuna for lunch today. I'm not sure my stomach can handle it.

I'm going to pass out for a few minutes before I have to be back at the Tanners.

Night, Journal. Well, I guess the sun's coming out now so…

Day, Journal.

PAT IS A COMPLETE AND TOTAL ASS.

Who the HELL reads a teenager's journal?! I am *so* pissed off I can't even put together enough words to form a rant! But I'm not so pissed off I won't try.

I don't care if you never had children of your own, and you're so ancient and decrepit you barely even recall your own childhood. You NEVER read someone's journal.

I don't care you've lived on an island for so long you've become completely alien to other civilized human life forms.

Never. Read. Someone. Else's. Journal.

Snooping around in my bedroom? Digging around to try to find out what I've been doing every day? Why not just *ask* me?

So, Journal, if you couldn't already tell, Pat heard me taking Auntie's car and went into my room to dig through my things. He found you, Journal. And read you.

So this morning, after my short nap, I went downstairs to an intervention—Pat and Auntie were looking at me firmly from the kitchen nook.

I was given the how-could-you-spy-on-those-people?! treatment. And, of course, the you-took-our-car-and-you're-only-fifteen! treatment.

I'm pretty sure I'm going to be grounded for the rest of my life on Orcas. My dad and Pat aren't super close—my father is almost seven years younger than Pat and has a strikingly different personality—so I doubt Pat will tell my parents anything. But with a crime so great maybe he will.

I felt seriously guilty until I started wondering HOW they knew I went to the Tanners'. They exchanged oh-crap-I-was-hoping-she-wouldn't-ask-that looks.

So then I found out what Pat had done. He said, "I was concerned about your well-being!"

Which. Is. Bull. He obviously just wanted to get dirt on me without having to confront me. If he was *so* concerned, he could have called me after I left the house last night, or stopped me from going, instead of digging around in my room to try to see why.

So that started yelling match number two, which ended with me stomping out of the house and slamming the door. And let me tell you, real heavy wooden doors slam *real well*.

I didn't have a car to drive, but there's a gas station a mile or so down the street. I bought some snacks and soda and ignored my cell phone buzzing away in my jacket pocket. And then I came across the most wonderful thing ever.

A bait and tackle box. This is a large fishing community, after all. The box wasn't huge. It only cost $10 and it had exactly what I needed on it—a lock.

So from now on, after I write in you, Journal, I shall be putting you into my new, nifty box and locking you away. With the only key hanging around my neck.

Problem solved.

I stalked back home, did NOT acknowledge Aunt or Uncle, and made my way to my room. Where I've been since.

So much for going to work today. I called and talked to Charlie, explaining to him there were some... family issues and I couldn't make it. He sounded understanding enough and asked if I'd be able to come in the rest of the week. Talking to Charlie cheered me up some. I couldn't help but feel sad I wouldn't see him at work today.

I can probably go make good with Auntie—it wasn't like SHE snooped around in my room without asking.

Thankfully, neither Pat nor Auntie decided to call the Tanners and tell them, though I suspect Pat wanted to. I don't plan on snooping again anyway—unless I find out something crazy while working.

I think I might go and talk to Auntie. I know she meant well. She was probably concerned about my safety. I did take her car without asking... and in the middle of the night... I'll just explain to her I was concerned about who I was working for, but now I don't have those concerns anymore.

Which is kind of a lie. But I want to continue working for them…

I'm hoping she'll understand, so I can at least get a ride to work and back. I should probably start making my own lunches, though, to lighten the load for her. I'm not sure I'd want to eat whatever Mr. Tanner makes. Yick.

Anyway, I better go. Time to lock you up, Journal.

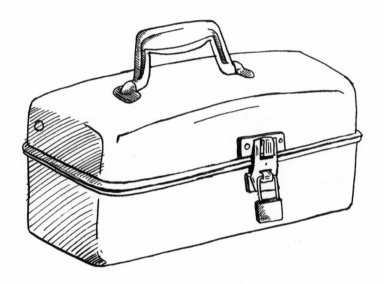

Last night I made good with Auntie. We had a pretty long heart-to-heart. I didn't tell her exactly what I saw at the Tanners', but I explained to her I was worried and wanted to make sure they weren't involved in anything illegal. I didn't want to ask them directly in case it was dangerous.

Which is technically true, but I may have left out some details.

We hit a couple rough patches when she tried to defend Pat. I understand he's her husband of thirty-something years, but she should understand I'm upset my own family went behind my back. It's true I shouldn't have gone snooping at the Tanners', but I never pawed through their personal belongings. And Pat is my uncle—he should have just asked me what was going on.

Auntie wanted me to talk it through with Pat, to tell him how I felt about it.

Like hell that's going to happen. I'm pretty sure our yelling match was a perfect example of our feelings.

Thankfully, Auntie backed off of that a bit, and we settled on an agreement she'd ask Pat not to snoop again, and I, in turn, wouldn't scream in his face.

I told her I'd start making my own lunches so she wouldn't have to worry about it, and hoped someone would still take me to work (and hopefully that person wouldn't be Pat).

I'm bringing you to work with me, Journal. We're going on a fossil walk today and I figure I'll have time to write something during lunch.

I'm off for now.

12:34 p.m.

It's been difficult to work with Mr. Tanner and Charlie... For some stupid reason, I hoped I could ignore everything and continue working like I had been. But when I'm face to face with them, all I can think about is breaking their trust and snooping on them—and seeing those lights.

There's no way I can bring it up. No situation lends itself well to, "I almost succumbed to raccoon-related injuries the other night. You know, when I was outside your window at 2:00 a.m.? So what's up with those lights? Are you dudes aliens or something?"

I keep thinking back on everything. Have they been lying to me? Where did they go on that week off? Why did they have a skull of something that should have been fossilized?

I watch them like hawks while we're here, but I can't bring myself to really look them in the eyes. I'm not sure if they can tell I've been acting strange, or if they've been acting strange. Given the looks Charlie's giving me, it's probably me that's acting odd. I may have Grade-A ninja skills when it comes to spying, but I can't keep myself from looking like a shifty-eyed loon after the fact.

Anyway, I just finished lunch and Charlie asked me to walk with him to another part of the fossil bed. Looks like we have some cataloging to do. Fun.

I'm the worst actress on the planet. First Pat realizes I'm up to something, and now this.

My little walk with Charlie ended up being a I-need-to-talk-to-you-away-from-my-grandfather kind of thing. We found an area that looked like it had been through a major rockslide. There were no homes around for miles, so it probably didn't affect anyone. A few feet away there was a hill that led down to a river below.

Charlie stopped and said, "We're far enough away now. We need to talk, Eliza." I wondered if I was about to get whacked… or shoved down a cliff or… something.

If I was, I was totally prepared to fight. I've gotten into a few scuffles with girls back home over stupid things, much to my mother and father's dismay. But this wasn't California and Charlie wasn't a middle school girl. I was pretty sure it'd be damn hard to take Charlie in a fight, especially without any sort of backup.

Well, I'm obviously still alive. No baseball bats to the head or anything.

He asked why I had missed work, and I told him the truth: I had gone against my aunt and uncle's wishes, and that my uncle destroyed some of the trust we had. And it had all blown up that day and I just couldn't make it.

There was no way I could tell him everything. I still feel like a jerk for not telling him how I peeked into his house that night. I'd been so pissed at Pat for breaking my trust, but now I'm breaking some of Charlie's trust.

Charlie looked at me like he was trying to tell if I was lying or not. I made a face at him. Immature, but I wanted to lighten some of the pressure.

He smiled but got quiet. He asked if I missed work because of the *Maiacetus* skull. He noticed I'd been quiet while working on it. I assured him it really was family issues that kept me away.

Something is going on, and I know something is going on, and he knows I know something is going onand neither of us are about to say anything.

I decided to ask the most important question.

"Is what you're doing illegal? Or dangerous?"

He laughed nervously. "No," he said. "Not illegal." But what about dangerous?

He said I should trust him. I said it was hard to trust someone I didn't know very much about. He said he understood.

I told him I didn't want to stop working for them, so he'd have the rest of the summer to prove he is trustworthy.

And that's where we stand right now. Even though things look the same I can tell everything from now on is going to be different. He confirmed they are keeping something from me.

I just wish he hadn't smiled that stupid grin of his.

Damn it all, I think I like him.

It's Friday! Technically I'm still at work, on my lunch break, but it doesn't

matter. It's Friday, ***that's*** what matters.

It's been a stressful week. I'm not sure what footing I'm on with the Tanners.

Charlie and I may have talked, but there's still a lot I don't know.

I'm happy to spend all weekend sleeping in. I know being home all weekend

with Pat might be unpleasant but I have a plan: ***ignore his entire existence.***

Today we've been looking at "bivalves throughout the ages." It's just as

exciting as it sounds. We looked at a number of them in the fossil bed yesterday,

and we're going over those today, as well as some others Mr. Tanner has collected

throughout his "travels."

What is a bivalve, you ask? If you care (and let's face facts here—I'm not sure

why you would):

A bivalve is a mollusc. A filter feeder. They look disgusting but they taste

good. There are a bunch of them living today, and many throughout the fossil

record. The family Veneridae alone has over 680 species in it.

We left off at the Jurassic period. The one I remember the most about is a

Mytilus bivalve Mr. Tanner recovered in southern Israel. If you don't know what

a mytilid is, there's no shame in that.

This species contains the well-known sea mussel people eat.

Mr. Tanner showed me a few other fossil specimens, and some of them are ancient. One Aviculopecten found near Ohio dated back to the Carboniferous—it was over 300 million years old.

I asked what the difference was between bivalves and brachiopods, because they look pretty similar most of the time. Mr. Tanner told me many things I can barely remember, but some of it had to do with the body structure, how the shells were attached to one another and how they functioned in opening the shell. There is also a difference between the "foot" of the mostly free-moving bivalves. The brachiopods rarely roam.

I'll take his word for it. I trust what he puts in front of me is a bivalve rather than a brachiopod.

I worked in the lime quarry with the brachiopods, and they just look like clams for the most part. Especially fossilized specimens, which are harder to tell apart because you can't pry one open to see inside.

And now, for some reason, I'm starting to crave seafood, even after working all morning with the little guys. You'd think that would put me off it forever, but no. Apparently, my hunger knows no bounds.

It was probably a bad idea to write before I ate anything. I'm going to go do that now. I'll get back to you later, Journal.

6:18 p.m.

I spent a few more hours working on my new, awesome, exciting bivalves project before Mr. Tanner said I was done. He said I could work on it during

BIVALVE SPECIES

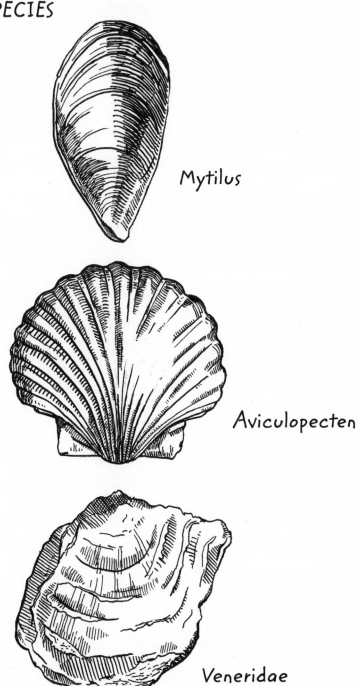

Mytilus

Aviculopecten

Veneridae

the weekend (that is SO not going to happen) or when I get back to work on Monday.

He did mention we'd be doing something bigger on Monday. Maybe I should work on it more this weekend… I'm still sleeping in, hell or high water.

After I was done for the day, Charlie said he wanted to show me some things. I accepted because (if you couldn't tell from me snooping around their house like a wannabe Navy SEAL) I am naturally a curious being.

We moved from working on the beachfront to the back porch. He asked me to wait there while he went inside, so I sat on the porch looking out over the water.

Normally I would have grown impatient, but it was such a nice day. The even heat of the midday sun became a light warmth. Everything was green—greener than usual with the sun's rays reflecting off the island. The water is never very bright or clear since these are Northwestern waters—they are certainly not the crystalline glass oceans of Hawaii, but the light reflecting off those murky blue-green waters was beautiful. The silvery sheen on the top of the water made the water look off-white in the distance, until something would break the waves, like a passing boat, a seal, or an otter.

I'm getting too attached to the island, especially knowing I'm only going to be here until the end of summer.

Charlie came back with a box full of more little boxes. He put it on the ground in front of us, took a seat next to me, and started to pull things out.

There were teeth from things I wouldn't have been able to guess, but I had Charlie there to fill me in. Most were land mammal carnivore teeth, but he had a few species of ancient horse teeth with him, too. One large megalodon tooth stood out among the rest of the sea life fossils and teeth. I'm terrified of sharks, and seeing how big their teeth were at one point in history gave me the willies.

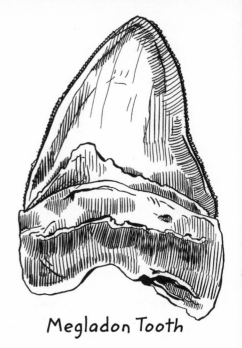

Megladon Tooth

He had plenty of bones mixed in, too—everything from mouse skulls to some sort of large reptile I didn't recognize. (It turned out to be *Erpetosuchus*, a weird crocodile-looking thingy.) One bone seemed to belong to some sort of monkey. When I asked about it, Charlie told me it was an *Australopithecus afarensis*, an early hominid, and most certainly not a monkey. He was very stern about the "**not** a monkey" part, and I laughed because he sounded like a younger version of his grandfather.

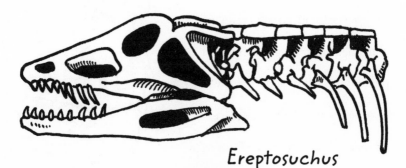

Ereptosuchus

Eventually, I started to notice little details on certain bones in his collection.

"It's not a fossil," I said, and I wasn't questioning him. Just like the *Maiacetus* skull, it was ancient but it wasn't fossilized.

"No, it's not," he said plainly, and didn't expand on it any further. He looked pleased, like he knew my growing knowledge reflected well on his teaching abilities.

Either he's in with some government program that clones ancient species, or he's got some sort of magical time traveling genie.

Maybe I haven't entirely worked out all the details yet.

"So this is your world," I said. He just nodded and smiled. I noticed how close he sat next to me.

"I like to think of it as a universal multiverse," he said. It was a good way of saying something while not saying anything at all, and judging by the grin on his face, he damn well knew it.

We continued to look through his collection, with him pointing out where things came from and what species they were. Whenever I noticed something was skeletal remains but was not fossilized, I prompted him to tell me how old it was.

The oldest fossil he had was a piece from an *Anomalocaris*, from the Cambrian.

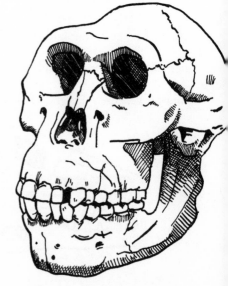

Australopithicus

Anomalocaris was a creature that would make shrimp cringe, turn tail, and hide. The oldest skeletal remains he had that weren't fossilized were from a type of Osteichthyes, a bony fish from the late Silurian period, nearly 420 million years ago. Unbelievable.

Anyway. Auntie's calling me for dinner, so, bye!

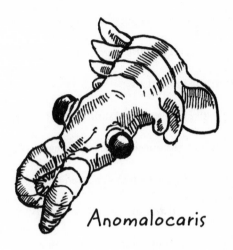

Anomalocaris

Today Auntie and I went into town to do some shopping. It was nice bonding

time, until she ran into a couple of her old friends at the fabric store. Noticing I

was bored, she suggested I head over to the bakery because they had really good

food. I wasn't super hungry, but it was better than hearing some ex-teachers talk

about the glory days.

I walked in to see a familiar lanky figure talking to the girl behind the

counter. I was shocked—I wasn't expecting to see Charlie outside the grip of his

grandfather, acting like a normal teenager.

The girl he was talking to was pretty, a natural pretty. She had dark brown

hair and a real tan (having lived my entire life in California, I can tell the

difference between a fake tan and a real tan). She was shorter than Charlie and

looked a few years older.

I could only see the side of Charlie's face, but I could tell he was enamored.

He had a big dumb grin on his face, and he was going on about baked goods

like he normally did fossils.

I wasn't jealous, but her food looked mediocre at best and she was annoying. And

she certainly wasn't making me self-conscious with her pretty hair or her nice jeans.

I was starting to rethink some of my earlier assumptions of Charlie, the

kindly nerd vibe he had going on. I just assumed, since I hadn't seen too many other teenagers around, Charlie liked Bigfoot style forest living and only ventured out once in a blue moon to startle hikers.

As I approached the counter, an older couple leaving the shop waved to Charlie. The woman said, "Nice seeing you again, Charlie! Tell Orville to take care of himself!" She turned to the girl. "Thanks again, Alex! It was delicious as always!"

This brought Charlie out of his spell. He turned to the couple. He was surprised to see me standing there. He glanced between Alex and me.

I sent him an awkward smile I'm hoping wasn't a grimace. "Hey, Charlie. This place any good?" I muttered, trying not to sound like a complete nutcase.

"Best bakery in town. My family runs it." Alex spoke up first. She was smiling.

"Well, doesn't that make you biased?" I wasn't sure where that came from. I felt really stupid for saying it. She blinked a few times.

"Yeah, I guess it does. Are you a friend of Charlie's? I haven't seen you around."

"New. Here for the summer. Working for his grandpa." I was hoping I didn't sound as petty as I felt, but that didn't stop me from strolling up to the counter and looking into the glass case. "**_Damn_**, those look tasty…" I trailed off, like a balloon out of a toddler's hand.

Alex laughed, pleasantly. Not mockingly. If she were from California it would have been a sneer and snort. But no. Just a happy chuckle. Washingtonians are **_weird_**.

Charlie looked like he was having trouble processing the situation. Maybe my idea he didn't have a ton of contact with people his own age was not totally off base. After he got over his moment of speechlessness, he asked if I wanted to go to an art show tomorrow.

So I forgive him. For what, I'm not sure.

I just got a call from Charlie. It's Monday, and apparently that means I'll be taking a boat out to Fossil Bay. Fossil Bay is on Sucia Island State Park, a short boat ride out from the north end of Orcas Island. Well, it should be a short boat ride, but since the Tanner house is near Fishing Bay, we'll be taking a trip up and around the east side of Orcas. If they had a car that could tow the boat across the small land expanse between this bay and the bay closest to Sucia, it wouldn't be a problem. But this isn't the case, so the trip is going to be a few hours longer than it needs to be. I'm just glad we aren't rowing all the way there.

This is why, after a lovely weekend of sleeping in, I am up at 5:00 a.m. and not very happy about it.

The rest of the weekend was… interesting. Meeting up with Charlie proved informative. He knows a lot about the island, like where the best shops and food places are. Ones that ***aren't*** a certain bakery.

The majority of the island's inhabitants seem to like Charlie and his grandfather, but I wonder if they've shared more than just a happy greeting in passing. The Tanners do a good job of fitting in just enough to not cause any alarm, but they're distant enough no one really seems to get too close.

I like hanging out with Charlie outside of work. It's taken away some of the drama and weirdness that's been hanging around these last few days.

Our trip to the art show was more nerve-wracking than pieces of molded clay should have been. One reason I enjoy art so much is that it's calming. This? Not so much.

We were only in the school auditorium turned art display (yes, there ARE kids on Orcas) for a few minutes before we ran into someone familiar.

Alex. Of course it was Alex. In fact, Charlie got the idea to come here FROM Alex.

Anyone with a brain could see Charlie's crush on her. I was annoyed this whole thing was her idea. We only had to chat with her for a moment though—I mean, Charlie only chatted for a moment—before she saw her friend and was pulled away. I did my best not to be awkward and attempted a sweet smile, which I'm sure was more of a grimace.

When she split I elbowed Charlie, perhaps a little harder than was appropriate. "So, what's with you and Alex?"

He gave me a confused look. "What do you mean? We're friends. That's all. She has a boyfriend." Then he shot me a sly smile and nudged me softly.

I couldn't help but blush. The existence of Alex's boyfriend was enough to put my mind at ease.

After the art show we went to one of those 1960s types of diners, and although the pink poodle skirts were a bit much, it had the best milkshake I've ever had in my life. Charlie told me it was one of his favorite places to get them, which prompted me to ask if he ever donned a black leather jacket and greaser hair.

After that we walked to an antique shop. Charlie talked about various items like he had been alive when they were in common use. I tried on old hats and Charlie said, "You might get lice." A mood killer if I've ever heard one...

Then, as though we hadn't done enough that day, we went to the beach. We didn't swim, but I was tempted. I was certain the moment a piece of seaweed wrapped around my foot I would've screamed bloody murder and jumped into Charlie's arms Scooby-Doo style–which would have been a bit awkward.

Charlie walked in and out of the water, with small waves hitting his sandals. He'd grin at me every once in a while and jump, splashing my pant leg with seawater like some sort of overgrown puppy. And, like a puppy, he was cute enough I let him get away with it.

It felt great to just kick back and have a good time during such a nice time of year. That was more how I imagined my summer vacation being—walking around in the sun, looking at wildlife, and chilling on the beach after browsing the local shops. Getting a cheap bite to eat and laughing about work or family or whatever came up.

After this weekend I feel really close to Charlie. You know, as a friend. Well, I guess as a friend. I like to think maybe he likes me a little, but it's probably just in my head. I still want to hang out with him, even if he won't tell me squat-diddly about whatever is going on with his family and these **not-fossils**.

So anyway. It's Monday. And we're going to Fossil Bay.

Charlie told me his grandfather took a smaller dinghy out to the island yesterday, so I'll be heading over with just Charlie and we'll meet up with Mr. Tanner once we get there. I'm kind of glad. Being up earlier than the birds and climbing into a boat with Mr. Tanner doesn't sound quite as fun as sailing with Charlie.

I've never seen Charlie captain a boat before.

There are sharks in those waters, aren't there? Sixgills and great whites, right?

11:53 a.m.

It's... ugh... almost noon. This is the worst idea I've ever had.

Charlie's probably a fine captain, so I guess I should calm down. He's worked around boats for years, though, admittedly, I doubt getting to know the very small stretch of water between Orcas and Fossil Bay takes a ton of seafaring know-how.

Ugh. I'm so tired of these stupid waves. This is the first time I've felt this seasick on a boat. I'm not going to try to write anymore. I'll just finish up when I get to Fossil Bay. It looks like Charlie's stopping the boat anyway... Ugh! I hope we didn't run out of fuel. There's no way I can row from here to Fossil Bay.

I'm going to see why we aren't moving anymore. I'll write in you later!

1:40 p.m.

He kissed me.

That is all.

Okay, no it isn't.

He stopped the boat so he could plant one on me. I'm not sure if that's romantic or badly planned. I was already feeling queasy from the waves.

After he kissed me, he looked upset. He asked if I was upset or grossed out since I looked a bit green.

I said I felt like I was gonna hurl, then realized he'd taken that the wrong way. I tried to wave him off, and my mad flails accidentally smacked into our lunches and knocked them into the water.

We were both apologizing at that point, frantically trying to assure the other of our own guilt. I started to laugh, because really, we're kind of morons.

Through my snorting laughter, I told him to try again on solid land, where I wasn't as likely to throw up on his shoes.

It was pretty cute. He went from confused to happy to awkward to blushing in about a half a second. He was windblown from the sea air—his hair sticking up in strange directions made me think of a ruffled seagull. He started the engine back up, which caused me to groan. I told him I was going below deck to lie down.

I hadn't been below deck before. It was surprisingly awesome. White and clean, with wooden paneling and a half-moon bed and another bench that could function as a pull-out bed. It looked like it could sleep four comfortably, and maybe more uncomfortably. I hadn't realized how nice their 24-foot Sea Ray was.

I heard the engine cut out again, and before I got comfortable Charlie popped his head down. His hair still looked like someone gave him a swirly and then let it dry that way. He handed me a glass of water and a pill for seasickness before heading up top and starting the engine up again. He's nice like that.

Before I knew it, I was fast asleep.

I wonder how many more times this summer I'm

going to start my entries with:

Pat needs to leave me the hell alone.

He stopped me on my way out this morning to

"talk" to me, and I really did not want to get into

another argument before work. I saw Auntie in the

kitchen, watching out of the corner of her eye, so I

just shrugged and nodded, figuring I could play nice for Auntie's sake. I followed

Pat outside.

He started by saying I was right, and he shouldn't have looked in my

diary. (Technically it's a journal, but I let that one slide since he was

apologizing to me.) But then he started on saying he thought I was right,

and I had good reason to be suspicious of the Tanners. *That* caught my

interest.

I wasn't sure what to say, because I wasn't sure how much he knew or why he

was suddenly so suspicious of them. Was it because of what I had written in my

journal, or was there a deeper reason he hadn't mentioned before?

I just told him that was old news, and I wasn't worried about them anymore

and he shouldn't be either.

He told me from the moment he dropped me off for the interview he felt something weird. He said he'd seen Mr. Tanner and Charlie around town a few times in the past, before I came to the island, and he thought there was something off about the two. Why hadn't they ever really gotten to know the other inhabitants of the island after living on Orcas for so long? Why was Charlie living with his grandfather instead of his parents? And why hadn't he enrolled in the local school system?

I have to admit: I've wondered the same things myself.

Pat told me he had wanted me to be careful around them from the very beginning, but felt now was the time to voice his concerns.

We weren't yelling, and even though I was worried about him getting caught up in the Tanners' business, I was somewhat pleased he apologized. He seemed to care about my well-being.

And then he said I should quit. I had a flashback to our first argument, when he got freaked out about me quitting. I bitingly mentioned that little incident, feeling my short temper fire up again. He told me in any other job he would have had a point, but "these people are strange."

I told him they just liked keeping to themselves, and that certainly wasn't *that* weird in an island environment. A lot of people moved out to islands to get away from the big cities like Seattle and Tacoma, or even out of Vancouver in Canada. Pat, though native to Washington, hadn't lived his entire life on Orcas Island.

I told him Charlie was my friend, and he told me I shouldn't hang around him anymore. "That boy is trouble," is what he said. I didn't realize we had transported ourselves into a '90s romantic teen drama and Pat was playing the part of the father who didn't like anyone or anything fun.

I said Charlie was a good person, and Pat didn't have to worry about anything. I was trying to keep myself from yelling, but I could feel my patience running low and my voice starting to rise.

Then he said he didn't want me dating Charlie.

I—I'm not even dating Charlie. I mean, there was that kiss yesterday on the boat... and when we got to the island yesterday, Charlie went in for another peck. I *had* told him to try again once we got to the shore, but then Mr. Tanner popped up out of nowhere like some crazy Sasquatch ghost, which caused me and Charlie to jump about a foot away from each other. Then I stuck my foot right into a sandy mud puddle.

I wasn't really sure what to say to Pat, so I told him Charlie and I were friends and he didn't have to worry about me coming home with a ring and a baby or anything.

The face he made still makes me smile.

It was about to get loud and screamy after that, so I was thankful Auntie popped her head outside and asked me if I was ready to go to work. I said yes, and grunted at Pat as I passed him.

I have a feeling he's going to keep bugging me about this until I quit or leave the island.

Now I'm at work, eating lunch at the Tanners' house. Earlier, I set up all my drawing things on the porch since it was nice out, ready to work on some of the things we looked at on Fossil Bay yesterday.

Charlie sat down close beside me and said hi. I told him my uncle thought he had ill motives and traveled the world collecting cat teeth.

He paused for a moment, and said, "I actually do have a few fossilized felid teeth…"

I'm certainly not looking forward to going home in a few hours. But right now, kicking back eating a sandwich while looking at the water, knowing I get to work with the most interesting people on Orcas Island, is enough to calm my nerves.

Another weird day, but those are so common maybe I should label weird days as the days when nothing out of the ordinary happens.

When I got home last night, Pat continued to try to convince me to quit working for the Tanners. Not surprising. I wasn't expecting him to drop the issue. Being stubborn runs in the family.

After I got home I plodded upstairs and threw my stuff into a pile on my bed, careful not to mess up any of the drawings I was working on. I went back downstairs, because I figured if I helped Auntie with dinner there was a smaller chance of Pat talking to me than if I was just sitting in my room drawing.

I was right, but dinner preparations lasted only 20 minutes before we were all seated at the dinner table. In California, I either stand and eat at the counter or take my food to my room. Here, there's no TV, and for a family with no children, they're surprisingly traditional about sitting down to eat at a table. It's not bad when we actually have something to talk about, especially a topic that isn't insanely awkward.

This wasn't one of those times. Pat poked and prodded at me to quit, restating his worries about the Tanners, especially Charlie.

Auntie didn't know what to do about all of it. I think she wanted to side with her husband and trust his instincts, but I was adamant there was nothing to worry about, so she mostly stayed out of it.

The next day, Pat was on the front porch when I darted by him to get to Auntie's car. He tried to say something, but I just waved and said I was already late and didn't have time to talk. (Kind of a lie. I was actually early, I just didn't want to start the day with complete suckitude.)

I found it odd Mr. Tanner was outside to greet me. Apparently, I would be working inside today. He led me through the house, to the same room where I had worked on drawing the *Maiacetus* skull. Immediately I was hit with the stench of sour milk stuffed inside a dead salmon that had been left out in the sun and rolled on by a wet dog.

There were four or five hulking... things piled on the table. I'm not sure if skeletons or carcasses is the best description. They looked like recently cleaned jumbo shrimps from hell, and I was pretty sure I had seen this particular kind of jumbo shrimp from hell before.

"*Anomalocaris?*" I asked. A frazzled Charlie emerged from behind the creatures.

"No, but close. Same family: *Anomalocaridid.*" Mr. Tanner said, and Charlie made a face. He was either upset Mr. Tanner beat him to the draw with the nerd info, or he just wasn't all that thrilled with the creatures themselves.

Charlie rounded the creatures and moved closer to me. I took three steps back and put up both hands. He looked upset by this, but I didn't really care.

"Nuh uh. No way you're coming near me **Chuck**. You smell like **them**." I gestured towards the creatures. I figured Charlie had the unlucky privilege of packing and unpacking the *Anomalocaridids*.

He huffed and ran a hand through his hair. I could only think, *Oh, his poor hair*. It was having a rough few days. Now it probably smelled like twice-over roadkill.

It took only a few moments for it to sink in that these things, if they were in the same family as *Anomalocaris*, were ancient and should have been long fossilized.

So. More *not-fossils*. Recently dead and smelling up the room.

"How old?" I asked, directing it towards Charlie. Mr. Tanner was there, but I felt odd asking him about it. He's scary sometimes, in a scruffy sea captain kind of way.

"Ordovician, so about 488 to 443 million years ago." Charlie gestured at them appreciatively before noticing some muck on his hands and wiping them on his pants. Gross.

I hadn't entirely memorized which dates applied to which animals, but I knew *Anomalocaris* was a main player in the Cambrian explosion. They were supposed to have died out by the end Cambrian.

I asked about this. Mr. Tanner replied before Charlie.

"We have no evidence *Anomalocaris* survived past the Cambrian. However, the *Anomalocarididae* family itself survived at least 33 million years after the end of the Cambrian."

Charlie cut in and said it surprised a lot of people that the family lived as long as it did. Apparently it was a recent discovery. I doubt any scientists would

Anomalocaridid

know how to react to a pile of carcasses that should have been fossilized on top of a table in the San Juan Islands.

"So," I asked, "what exactly *are* they if not the *Anomalocaris* I'm familiar with?"

"*Laggania cambria*," Charlie replied. Pretty name for a giant demon shrimp.

"Can you draw them?" Mr. Tanner asked.

"Of course," I said.

They left, probably to bathe in tomato juice, and for the next few hours I was all by myself in that little room with those horrible-smelling *not-fossils*.

When I got home later, I immediately ran upstairs to take a bath myself. Being in that room for so long left my hair smelling more than a little fishy.

In the bath I contemplated the best way to approach the subject of what was coming next: The Tanners asked me to join them on a two-day camping trip.

Mr. Tanner said knowing Orcas Island better would be beneficial to my work, and a camping trip would help me to familiarize myself with the landscape. Apparently, I need to be able to prove myself competent when it comes to camping and the outdoors. "Just in case," Mr. Tanner had said.

Unfortunately for me, I have to tell Pat and Auntie tomorrow I'll be going on a camping trip with the people Pat distrusts so much.

I'm sure this will go over well.

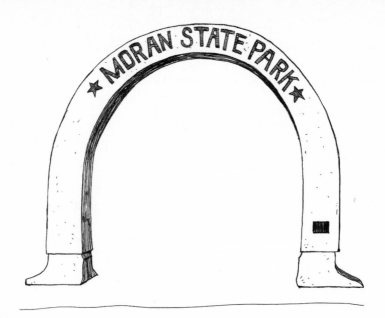

 August 4 — 8:20 a.m.

Moran State Park, here I come!

It took quite a bit of convincing on my part to actually get permission to go.

Pat wasn't thrilled with the idea of me going into the woods with the Tanners for

a few days. I think a part of him thinks I won't come back.

Auntie had some problems with it, too. Teenagers alone in the forest? I can

kind of see her point.

Not that she has anything to worry about. Mr. Tanner will be there. Even if

Charlie and me were at a point where I'd even think about—well— let's just say

there's no way in hell I'd even think about it with Mr. Tanner in the next tent over.

That is basically what I told Auntie (without certain implications), and after

assuring her there would be adult supervision, I eventually got the okay. That's all I needed—I don't care if Pat throws a fit the entire time I'm gone. He's not my ride.

I grabbed what I needed. You know, the essentials: sleeping bag, tent, flashlight, clothes, more clothes, drawing supplies, toothbrush, cell phone, iPod, large knife, makeup. And with that I was ready to go.

I'm in the car right now. Auntie's going to drop me off at Moran's arch gate. I'll call Charlie once I get there so he can meet me. Moran State Park is over 5,000 acres of land, and I really don't want to trek though all of it to find their campsite. (That, and I don't want to carry my own luggage.)

I see the white arch, so I better get going. Write in you later!

2:00 p.m.

Okay, this is kind of awkward.

Mr. Tanner is… absent. I'm not sure when he'll get here and neither is Charlie, apparently.

Charlie picked me up at the gate and drove us to the campsite. Mr. Tanner wasn't there, so I figured he was out gathering firewood or something. Yeah, no. Charlie told me it was going to be just me and him. For now. I'm guessing he'll be back before dinner, but I have no idea with that man. He's like a phantom. Charlie said he "went fishing" but it's the middle of the day. Not entirely prime fishing time.

So in case Mr. Tanner does spend the night elsewhere, I'll be sleeping with my knife very close. What if there's a wild boar attack? Or what if Charlie gets any fresh ideas?

Charlie just suggested going hiking.
There's a small waterfall nearby, so I
guess I'll be going for now.

Lord, if Pat or Auntie find out
there's no Mr. Tanner in sight, I am
SO screwed.

9:00ish? p.m.

Mr. Tanner finally showed up.
When he popped out of the bushes
and scared the living daylight out of me, Charlie just said, "Cataloging?"

Mr. Tanner's reply was a solemn nod, a glance in my direction, and a heavy
sigh.

But this was after the day's excitement.

We went fishing! (No sign of Mr. Tanner at all.) It was catch and release,
but it was still fun. The fish were pretty active as the sun was going down,
surprisingly enough. Maybe because there wasn't anyone else around, so the lake
was untouched.

The hike to the lake was nice, too. I'll never get over just how beautiful the
scenery is around here. The sounds, the greens, and the smell. I'll miss all of this
when I go home, back to the smell of pavement and dust. In California, the
grass and flower beds constantly need watering to keep them from dying. Here?
Green year round. The grass stays green longer because of the rain, and the forest

floors are so thick and deep it's impossible to see ten feet in front of you because of the foliage and primeval-looking ferns that unfurl in spring and summer.

I'm not really sure how I'll go back to the monotony of home after this, but I'll enjoy it while I can. I should be paying more attention to the campfire than my journal.

Mr. Tanner is off doing lord-knows-what again, and I think Charlie wants something. He keeps saying "So..." and trailing off. He either wants to mack or talk, and I probably shouldn't be writing in my journal while doing either.

2:00 a.m.

I'm going to try and sleep, though I know I won't have much luck. Charlie told me it was unfair to keep secrets from me, given how close we've become.

At that moment, Mr. Tanner spirited out of nowhere and startled the two of us with a very harshly toned, "***Charles***." It wasn't even more than Charlie's name, but it shut him up quick. His mouth snapped closed faster than a bear trap.

Charlie shot me this look like, ***I'm sorry, please don't ask***. Of course I respected his wishes and didn't ask. And not just because Mr. Tanner still freaks me out sometimes.

However, looking over and seeing my black beanie lying carelessly over my travel bag gave me a new idea. A horrible, terrible idea that would probably destroy the small amount of trust I might've gained in the last few weeks.

I'm still in my tent and I haven't heard the Tanners stirring yet. I got a few hours of sleep, but only because of pure exhaustion from yesterday's hiking and fishing. Otherwise I was up thinking most of the night.

I didn't really go into detail before. Like I said in my last entry, it's just too risky. I stayed up all night thinking about my plan. A good part of that planning involved thinking up a totally kickass name for it too.

I'm thinking **Operation Tyrannosaurus Rocket Launcher**.

So, obviously something strange is going on, and that something is so severe that even though I've worked for the Tanners for awhile they aren't willing to tell me outright what it is. At least Mr. Tanner isn't.

Yet, it's not as if they could think I'm completely unaware something is up. They're the ones giving me all the **not-fossils**. They'd have to figure me for a complete dunce if they thought I wouldn't **kind of** start to question them.

Charlie told me a bit about his family last night, and his grandfather was there. But I got the feeling he was speaking partial truths. He might be a bit bashful and nerdy at times, but he's got a smooth tongue when it comes to the subtle art of deception.

His parents lived in New York—they moved there for business when Charlie was young. For many years, Charlie spent the school year with his mother and father, returning to Orcas Island for the summer to live with his grandfather.

When he turned 13, he started spending the school year here on Orcas and spending the summer with his parents. Eventually, he'd only spend a month with his folks back East. He missed them, he said, but this wasn't because of an affinity for Washington or because he just liked spending time with his grandfather. He was a protégé and was being trained constantly so he could eventually inform his own children and possibly his grandchildren. I couldn't help but question, **About what?** as if there wasn't something fishy going on. I wasn't certain fossil hunting was a family business outside the Tanners.

They were always perfecting the art, finding the right locations—intricate work for a bunch of old bones. Charlie hinted that the pay off was usually fairly substantial, which grabbed my attention.—

I asked how far back in his family's history they'd been fossil hunters, and he said as far back as he knew. They have records of family members since as early as the 1700s in ugly old khaki's out in the middle of all kinds of terrain. I remembered some of the older photos in their home, thinking about how sometimes the backgrounds looked positively alien.

I glanced down at his left shin, which his baggy shorts left uncovered. There was a sizable scar across it, and I thought back to one of our days off when Charlie joked about how he got it. "*Velociraptor*," he told me. "Smart, but nasty little buggers."

I started to wonder about the fossils. I started questioning the partial truths that may have come from either of the Tanners' mouths. I had laughed many things

Ordovician Life

off, taking them as Charlie's odd sense of humor. But now, with the mounting strangeness of everything, I have to ask myself if I really believe that anymore.

Mr. Tanner is an expert fossil tracker, and he passed along his know-how to Charlie. Maybe it's nothing more than them just being wonderfully lucky and horribly vague. The most plausible answer is the simplest one, right?

On the other hand, if you have the skeletal remains of something that should be fossilized, the most logical assumption would be that the creature was still alive—or a hoax.

That thought made my blood run cold. I really like the Tanners, so even contemplating the idea that all of this could be some sort of elaborate hoax is unpleasant. But, it's possible, right?

It'd make more sense than some silly, sci-fi geek's ramblings over time travel or something crazy like that.

I want to believe in Charlie, though.

That night, as I made my way to my tent I noticed Mr. Tanner watching me, before standing up and walking past me, into the forest. I felt like a deer in headlights. He had to know I suspected something unusual about him, about both of them.

As he walked passed, he spoke to me too quietly for Charlie to hear: "You're welcome to try."

He vanished into the forest, calling back to Charlie about going to get kindling. I looked down nervously at the large pile of kindling we already had.

His words left me very confused and alone with my thoughts, a dangerous thing in and of itself. Later, I worked out he meant, "You're welcome to try and figure us out. If you can."

Well, you've got yourself a deal.

Velociraptor

I know I didn't write anything more yesterday, but I was exhausted. After I got up and helped make breakfast, Charlie and I spent all day hiking. Mr. Tanner was still at the campsite when we left. He nodded at us both as we walked off down the trail. It was a good way of ignoring all the drama that was sure to rear its head again.

Moran State Park is lovely and lush. It was really easy to forget all my worries and problems, even if only for a few precious moments. And that lasted about five minutes.

Charlie brought it up again when we got back to the campsite, around 7:30 p.m. His grandfather was gone once again.

As we grilled up some more hot dogs from the cooler, Charlie sat down beside me, pretty close as always. (This was his signature move: sit as close as possible, make casual conversation, and act like he's not trying to smell my hair. Which, after being in the forest for a day, probably didn't smell awesome.)

He said, "I'm glad you came with us to…" he made a vague gesture to the scenery– "you know, here." I'll take that as a good sign?

I said he was my meal ride. He laughed, but he looked like he was trying to tell if I was joking or not.

"So…" He was looking at the fire and avoiding eye contact.

"Calm down, Charlie," I said, "You don't have to tell me everything right now." And it's true, because I was going to figure it out for myself.

He nodded and muttered "Thanks, but..." under his breath before looking back at me. He has pretty eyes. I think his eyelashes are longer than mine, which is totally unfair. "I was actually going to ask you about... the situation between us. I figured you already knew I had a crush on Alex?" he said, his voice low and uncertain.

"Before you got here, of course," he tacked on quickly.

"Yeah," I said, a bit caught off guard. "You're kind of obvious about it when you're around her. But, it's okay–I mean–whatever this is, it's just a summer thing right?"

I had all sorts of unhappy thoughts bubbling up inside me. Jealous, angry stupid thoughts that had no place in my head. I was trying to convince myself that what we had wasn't going to last. Leaving at summer's end would end it pretty definitively, if I didn't manage to screw up whatever weird pact I made with the Tanners first. Which was highly probable.

He smiled dryly. Time to change the subject, and my nose picked up the perfect cover.

"Chuck, your weenie is on fire."

He choked on air before he noticed his hot dog had burst into flames. It was now a lovely charcoal-black color.

Mr. Tanner had misted into the campsite like a phantom as always. He barked out a quiet laugh. That was the first time I ever heard him laugh, come to think of it.

After we extinguished the hot dog, Charlie attempted to tell a ghost story that involved a hook and bear. When it was over Mr. Tanner said, "Charles, that was quite possibly the worst campfire story I have ever heard."

That got me cackling, and Charlie's angry/embarrassed look made me laugh even harder.

"How could a bear attach a claw hook to its tail!?" I said.

Mr. Tanner piped in with, "Come to think of it, I bought Charles a teddy bear when he was a child and he was absolutely terrified of it."

I was laughing so hard I had to stop myself from sliding off my seat.

After that we had a pretty good night, laughing and joking accompanied by some light cuddling before going to sleep. (Of course, this was after Mr. Tanner went to bed. No cuddling around Grandpa.) It was obvious that Charlie and I were ignoring our earlier awkwardness, and we both knew it. But bringing it up again was out of the question, for now anyway. I slept pretty well until a raccoon attacked the side of my tent. What is it with me and raccoons?

This morning I had a very healthy breakfast of Cheerios and sugar, then Charlie asked if I wanted to hike to Summit Lake and take a canoe out on the water. He seemed to notice Mr. Tanner watching us with sharp eyes, so he extended the invitation to his grandfather. Mr. Tanner politely declined. He said he had some business with the park ranger and would be gone most of the day.

I hadn't been in a canoe before, so I was all for it, but only after I hit the nearby shower. I needed to *not* have a layer of dirt on my skin.

The rockiness of the vessel threw me off at first, but I was on the swim team when I was younger, so I wasn't really worried. Then Charlie told me there is such a thing as lake sharks, but I needn't worry about any here. (Thanks, Chuck. You're *real* good at calming someone down.)

We got back to our campsite around 7:00, exhausted and damp from the canoe. I told him if we ate hot dogs again I'd shove them up his nose. We ended up having freeze-dried camping food. He ate some sort of chicken and rice dish, and I had lasagna. For freeze-dried

food in a bag, it was actually pretty good... or I might have just been really, really hungry.

It started to get windy out after dinner, which was a convenient excuse to sit close together. At one point, he put his arm around me. A romantic gesture, but I was well aware he hadn't showered that morning like I had.

"Is Eliza your full first name?" he asked. I guess I looked at him oddly, because he continued. "I mean, is your first name Eliza, or is that short for Elizabeth?"

I shook my head. "Nah, just Eliza. My mother's side of the family is third generation Spanish. She had a relative... great-aunt or something named Eloisa Eufémia. My middle name is Eufémia, too, so that's how I got my name. Eliza Eufémia Walcott."

He smiled. "Know any Spanish?"

"Only the curse words."

"My middle name is Augustus."

I broke out laughing. "Charles Augustus Tanner?"

He pinched my arm with the hand that was around my shoulder. "Better than Eufémia!"

"Not by much!"

It was nice out here. It was nice being here...

"Eliza, we have another pretty big project coming up. I was wondering if you wanted to work late next week. We can have dinner together at the house and of course, you'll get overtime, it's just that, Grandpa and I– well, you too– have a ton of stuff to work on.

I just nodded and smiled.

I know I said I didn't plan on snooping again but this seems to be too good of a chance to find out what the Tanners are hiding.

So much happened today. I'm not sure where to start...

Charlie and I packed up our stuff pretty early since checkout was at noon. Mr. Tanner said he was taking his truck back to the house to drop off the equipment. I wasn't aware he had brought any equipment besides the few notebooks he had with him.

Charlie dropped me off at home, Pat watching from the porch with eagle eyes. Charlie helped me carry my things to the porch. (I was more than capable, but it was sweet he tried. He only stumbled a little.) Charlie knows Pat doesn't approve of him, so I'm sure he was trying to make a good impression. He smiled at Pat and said a merry hello. Pat grunted in response.

Auntie heard the car pull up and the footsteps on the porch and poked her head outside. Being the nice one, she invited Charlie in for a bite to eat, since it was around lunchtime. I think she was curious about the motives behind the camping trip. I was, too, truth be told, but I just figured it was some sort of strange company picnic.

She asked where his grandfather was. I snapped to attention and said, "He's back at their house," before Charlie could say anything. Auntie and Pat were already on such uneven ground with the Tanners, and Charlie was trying to make nice. I didn't want to ruin everything by saying, "Oh yeah, no, he was, like, barely even there. We pretty much had free reign the entire time. Even at night."

It wasn't like anything happened... nothing **bad** anyway. But they'd—Well, Pat would completely flip out and Auntie wouldn't be able to defend me if it looked like I knowingly went camping alone with Charlie. They wouldn't look fondly upon Mr. Tanner leaving two teenagers alone as much as he had, which would strain relations even further, so when Pat wasn't looking I shot Charlie a look that said, "If you say anything more, it's **your** funeral." He seemed to get the signal.

Hearing us talk about hiking and our canoe trip over lunch seemed to entertain Auntie. I'm sure Pat would have enjoyed hearing about it, too, but he was still being a jerk and refused to come eat with us.

After eating, Charlie said he should get back to his own house because his grandfather might need help preparing work for tomorrow. We said goodbye, and Auntie sent him off with a small tin of cookies.

Charlie tried to say something nice to Pat as he passed him, but Pat just grunted again.

It wasn't even a full ten minutes after Charlie left before Pat came inside and gave me the news: He asked one of his buddies who ran a small grocery and bait store to get me a job. I could start working there tomorrow. (I heard Auntie sigh somewhere in the kitchen. She knew how I'd react to this—not very well.)

I gave him the best straight-faced glare I could and told him I already had a job. One that paid pretty well at $11 an hour. I know a few people back in California who have been working for years who barely make $11 an hour!

Then his cell phone rang. He grunted his greeting, a few yeses and handed it to me. I looked at it like it was diseased before I grabbed it. A small, squeaky "Hello?" emerging from the phone made me put it to my ear.

It was my mother.

Of course it was my mother. There's no way Pat **couldn't** get every single human I know involved in this. Hell, scratch "human." Soon he'll probably be forcing me to talk out life lessons with our neighbor's dog, Killer the Pomeranian.

"Heeey Mom... How's Tampa?" I shot Pat a look before I moved into the kitchen to talk. Auntie watched me from the table.

"Good," she said. "Very hot, though. Your father hates it, of course." My dad and Uncle Pat were both born here in Washington. There was a part of California living my father never grew accustomed to: the heat. Anything over 80 degrees Fahrenheit completely melted his will to do anything.

I chatted with my dad for a while before he handed the phone back over to my mom. I hadn't called them since I got here and I felt kind of guilty about it.

I suppose there are some times the 8:00 p.m. "Hope u had a good day. Love u," text message just doesn't cut it.

Eventually the conversation turned to areas I wished she wouldn't inquire about, but my mother felt it was her life duty to ask: "Meet any boys?"

I responded something about only being here for the summer and how could I *possibly* want to get involved with anyone?

Then she asked about work. I said it was good and I was really enjoying myself, and it was interesting and fulfilling.

"Good, good. I hear you haven't been getting along very well with your uncle, though. Is there a problem?"

I made a face, which was Auntie's signal to leave the room. "We wouldn't have a problem if he'd keep his nose out of my business and stop being so damn paranoid about everything." It was hard to say that much with a shred of force behind it, honestly. As of the last few days I've had my own paranoid delusions to chew on.

"Language. Well, I've heard your uncle's side of it, too. I think you need to be more considerate of his feelings"— like he has any—"and realize he's just looking out for you. I'm not going to tell you to quit your job because I trust your judgment… most of the time. Just try to understand his perspective, too, okay?"

I grunted. It wasn't hard to tell the family resemblance between him, my father, myself, and even my Nana when it came to being aggravated. Our language system seemed to have evolved into a series of grunts.

I've said it once; I'll say it again: I wouldn't have a problem with Pat if he didn't keep going behind my back about things. If he's concerned, he should just ask me. I don't like having him meddle in my business. Maybe he does have reason to be suspicious of the Tanners... lord knows it goes without saying that even I'm a bit curious about them too. But that doesn't mean he has to act like a complete jackass about it.

Ugh. Anyway. I need to go calm down. Maybe I'll walk down to the shop and back.

Bye for now, Journal.

In Irvine, walking a few blocks is an easy way to clear my head. Dad always warns me it's dangerous, but I get to know people I wouldn't have otherwise. I think that's safer than having no connections at all, right?

But that isn't to say I don't like having moments of downtime. It always amuses my parents if I go over to a friend's place, or they come to mine, and one of us will be watching TV and the other playing games on the computer, barely speaking to each other—it's still bonding, I swear!

Ugh. Don't mind me rambling. I'm just thinking everything over.

Today's the day I'll be springing the idea of spending a few days working late at the Tanner's on my Aunt and Pat. I would have kept putting it off, but it was more than obvious that Charlie wanted me to get the A-OK as early as possible.

Work has been mundane, but I just keep getting that mounting feeling that something big is happening, and I'm the last to know. That never seems to be an oddity in my life. My parents are always springing things on me at the last minute, and my friends keep secrets. Like when Maria didn't tell me that Rachel told Jen that Brea was hanging out with Candice because Caroline was dating that one Finnish exchange student. Written out it now occurs to me how boring that sounds.

Sometimes I feel like I have more barely-know-you friends, than anything real. Maybe because it seems like the people I'm closest to don't trust me with anything.

Every once in a while I'll think to myself maybe I want to live here, on Orcas Island. I mean, it's a beautiful area, but then I'd be leaving my friends and part of my family behind in California. But then I feel like, "So what?"

Though, would I really be escaping any of that here? Pat doesn't trust me, Charlie and Mr. Tanner are keeping secrets.

I know a lot of people leave home after high school to go to college, but some of the best colleges on the West Coast are in California. There's not even a college on Orcas Island... I'd have to catch the ferry every day to classes if I wanted to go!

That is, if I go to college at all. Mom would kill me if I didn't, but maybe I could work long term with the Tanners. Not that I could really live on an island by myself on just $11 an hour... maybe I could live with the Tanners? They have a big house—no, that would be *really* awkward. But what am I saying?! I still have two more years of high school!

Anyway. Speaking of the Tanners, today at work I was given the most exciting task of all!

Drawing more freaking brachiopod fossils.

Brachiopod

I'm really hoping that this wasn't Charlie's idea of a big project. Maybe Mr. Tanner is making sure I didn't get rusty after a weekend of not drawing anything. Or maybe it was some sort of punishment, though I have a sneaking suspicion any punishment Mr. Tanner would hand out would be far more severe.

I may sound like I'm complaining, but it really wasn't that bad a day. Charlie was there helping organize the fossils, so I at least had someone to talk to, even if he was going into super-geek mode and rambling off things faster than I could process.

I'll admit it: it's actually kind of endearing. I can honestly say, a lot of the time, even when he's being a dork, I have better conversations with him than I do with my friends.

Sometimes it feels like I have a bunch of friends, but no real best friends. Getting along this well with Charlie is nice. I wonder if he has a computer. I'd like to stay in touch with him when I go home. You know, apart from just cell phones.

I mean, if my relationship with Pat never recovers, I may not come back again. The thought kind of makes me sick. I *really* like it here.

Maybe I could come back next summer and then I could move near here after school? I could get an apartment in Seattle and go to University of Washington. That way I could still come visit Charlie, but appease my mother and still go to school. All I know is, I want to come back to Washington.

And I can't forget about what coming back to Orcas would mean. I'd continue to face the mysteries of the Tanners, but more importantly, what would become of me and Charlie? The relationship is bound to change more and more.

Anyway, speaking of Charlie, I should probably go tell Auntie and Pat soon about working late. Wish me luck, I'll report back in before I go to bed.

9:23 p.m.

Okay, THAT did not go as well as planned.

Apparently I can go into the woods with the Tanner's alone, but staying late at their house, minutes away by car is essentially the same as me saying I want to run away with the circus.

I tried to be as diplomatic as possible. I started in a real smooth, NPR-esque voice and led with, "The Tanners and I have an inordinate amount of work this week and they have asked that I stay late for a few nights." I went on to say that I would be eating dinner there for the next three nights, but the bonus was I would be getting paid overtime.

Auntie talked about the dinners she had planned and Uncle Pat just grunted and said he did not trust the Tanner's motives. We went back and forth for a while and just when things were about to get real heated, just after Uncle Pat said, "This was probably that Tanner boy's idea," Auntie Gin came to my rescue once again. She said that I was actually being responsible by taking on more work and that there would be nothing more valuable for the start of my adult life than a strong resume as a teenager. Pat eventually gave his permission, but he grunted and grumbled something about there being no future in drawing extinct animals and that I was deluding myself in thinking that there were any other employers like the Tanners anywhere else on the planet.

For once, I actually agree with Uncle Pat. But that doesn't mean I don't still want to work late at the Tanner's.

Night, Journal.

When I arrived for work this morning, I was practically skipping, feeling awfully happy with myself and my career path.

It wasn't often I actually worked inside the house. Part of the porch was protected from wind gusts coming off the water, and in the summer weather it made more sense to be outside rather than cooped up in a stuffy old house. However, this day when I made my way back to our usual meeting space there was a note on the table.

"I'm in the mail room, come on in. -Charlie"

I frowned. His handwriting was weird. Like old fashion calligraphy.

I found Charlie in the same room I'd drawn the *Bison antiquus* skull, going back and forth between cataloging mail and the brachiopod work we had done earlier. He seemed happy enough, though a bit distracted when I leaned up against some sort of display case and told him I was cleared to work late for the next few days.

"I'm glad you can stay, but it's not going to be very exciting, like a house party or a dance. Not like I've ever been to either one of those," he muttered flipping through letters, pausing every once and awhile to toss out an "INSTANT WINNER. CLAIM NOW" flyer. "Unless you count the annual rock and gem show as a party."

I was starting to unpack my own work supplies when I heard him, and snorted. "Yeah, well you didn't miss out on much. Screaming girls, power plays for attention, doofy guys trying to be cool and more screaming. At least that's the way it's been with my friends."

I glanced over to see Charlie looking at me strangely, and I paused in my preparations, letting my art book slip back down into my canvas bag. "What? Do I have Cinna-Plenty-Munches on my face?"

He shook his head, his hair a bit shaggier than when we first met.

"It's nothing. It's just I haven't heard you talk about your friends before really. I think I've heard you mention a couple names, but not really anything beyond that." Long fingers flipped through a couple more letters, "I guess when I first saw you I figured you'd be the—*so and so did this, so and so did that*—you know, that type."

I was tempted to hurl an eraser at him. "That's kind of prejudice isn't it? I'm a teenage girl, therefore I must talk constantly?"

Suddenly he wasn't focused on the mail anymore, but looking at me like a deer on the highway would look at an oncoming semi-truck.

"Uh, no. I mean. You do talk a lot. Just not about your friends. Not that girls have to talk more than boys, it's just that you happen to– which is fine and I'm okay with it. In fact I like your voice, so it's really not that big–" Charlie was talking so quickly his words were starting to run into one another and his voice went up an octave.

I held out a hand to silence him, it was just too sad to let continue.

"I'm just not the type to keep close friends, okay? Period." I said sharply and instantly regretted how much I sounded like Pat just then.

We sat in silence for a few seconds before Charlie said quietly, "If I could, I'd love to have close friends. Best friends even." I breathed out my nose, before responding.

"Well, why don't you?" but it was a stupid question. I wasn't sure what was controlling Charlie's life, but it was apparent it didn't allow him many liberties when it came to having a social life.

"I just... can't. But you can! You go to a normal school, in a normal town with a normal family! Bu-"

"Normal?!" I gasped, my voice raising, "I live in an apartment complex where my next door neighbor practices voodoo! My mom and dad shipped me off to Washington so they could go to Florida. My first pet-sitting duty was watching chickens! *In an empty swimming pool!*" I knew I was just getting irrational and annoying by the end, but it didn't really matter to me. "And my parents are *never* around, even during the school year." I became aware that I had snapped a pencil in my fist, and I was breathing fiercely.

Charlie was biting his lip, and looked a bit sheepish. I knew my life wasn't bad. I knew my parents loved me. I didn't really even mind the voodoo or the chickens. Lord knows my experiences with the Tanners were eighty times as weird as anything I had dealt with in my life up until that point. I'm sure

Charlie's life was a boiling cauldron of freaky. I had never heard much about his parents, or even Mr. Tanner's wife. Which was a thought that had never occurred to me until now.

"Voodoo, huh?" Charlie said blankly, and I snorted, tension easing out of the room.

"Sorry, it's just, you know. More that I haven't really met anyone I wanted to have that tight a friendship with. It seems like everyone has something they want to keep from everyone else, and it's hard to get past that," I said, sighing and digging out another pencil. It wasn't as though I didn't have friends, I thought. Or that I never talked about them.

I thought back to a time when Gwen left a garter snake in Manny Prince's bag, and smiled at the memory of his shrieking wails.

Charlie nodded, in a **tell me about it** way. Were his secrets so strange or severe that they really kept him from having any friends?

My mind shifted to Alex and the couple at the bakery, and I realized that everyone I had seen Charlie around had good thoughts about him. But none of them really knew much about him either. The few times I had seen Alex she seemed to believe I was closest to Charlie. I was starting to think she was probably right.

It made me all the more eager to discover any and all of Charlie Tanner's secrets. I felt like I owed it to the Charlie I had seen moments ago. The boy that desperately wanted close friends of his own.

It was turning more into a quest than just a girl snooping about in someone's house.

The rest of the day progressed normally, and I was glad to see our earlier tiff did nothing to quell my overtime. Charlie didn't bring up the borderline fight we had, and Mr. Tanner seemed more amused than usual.

I glanced at the old photographs on the wall as I walked down the hallway on my way out of the house. Wondering what I might find in the many rooms I had never seen.

August 11 — 4-something o'clock

I've been working the better part of the day on drawing various

brachiopods and Charlie has left to make some tea and get us a snack.

At lunch he gave me a brief tour of more of the Tanner house than I had seen

before. I'll give you a quick run down.

He showed me the second floor. Where I had never been, in fact I hadn't even

seen the main staircase leading to the upper stories. Turns out that past the room

where I had my "interview," and through another room was a cast iron spiral

staircase. I had never seen a room specifically for a staircase before, but now it

made sense as to why I never caught a glimpse before.

Charlie let me see his bedroom on the tour, and I was happy to see it was

a fairly normal teenage room, but instead of rock and roll or sport posters

he had a very old painting of a lighthouse, "Montauk lighthouse, my Great

Grandmother painted it," and a poster of New York City.

Across from his was the master bedroom; Mr. Tanner's. It took me a moment

to realize that Mr. Tanner's room had to have been in the turret of the house.

Fancy, I thought to myself.

The Tanner's house was large, and seemingly had more rooms than I could

count, but there was no way all of those rooms could be full size. The vast

majority must be more like walk-in closets than living space.

He showed me a guest bedroom, which was a bit dim and didn't appear to be very well furnished. The bed was made, but the blankets looked old. Clean, but old.

I turned around and shrieked at the picture on the wall.

Charlie had been loitering at the room's entrance, but ran in the second I yelled. I pointed a shaking finger at the picture.

"What? It's just a Harlequin. You don't like clowns?" He wasn't even trying to contain his mirth.

That clown seemed to be following me around! I thought bleakly to the same picture I left in my Aunt's study when I first arrived here in Orcas.

"Harlequin is a very old clown, dating back to medieval Italy, or some historians say even earlier, to ancient Mediterrania." I whipped my head around and Mr. Tanner was standing in the doorway. "A symbol of jesters, individuals who could unite both the powerful and the poor, yet never fit truly into the worlds of either. Harlequin became a calling card for some individuals. If you saw his picture in a home, you'd know you had an ally."

Why would my relatives have the picture, I wondered. And wasn't Harlequin the name for trashy romance novels? I thought the name sounded familiar from books my mom liked to read– to get her mind off work she used to say. Either way, they probably just picked it up at a yard sale or something, and pushed the thought from my mind.

That was the end of the tour and I followed Charlie to finish that day's work. It wasn't even close to dark out yet, but we decided to work in the mail room regardless. Might have been because of the hummingbird size mosquitoes that come out around dusk.

Dinner was amazingly surreal. I'm not sure what I was expecting, maybe a fancy Victorian-style dining room with low hanging chandeliers and the full princess treatment or something. But no, we ate actually in the kitchen. Charlie slouched over the counter, me on a stool at the kitchen island, and Mr. Tanner gazing out the small kitchen window.

We ate in silence, except when Mr. Tanner would shoot a dirty look at whoever was eating the loudest.

Usually me.

I never heard any mentions of TV time, or anything most people would consider normal after a meal. In fact we barely even spoke.

It was more uncomfortable than the camping trip by about one billion times.

I kind of felt like I was encroaching in on their space, and Charlie may have been guilty about inviting me over in the first place, and I was fairly certain Mr. Tanner enjoyed the sweet taste of awkward silence.

It didn't take long for Mr. Tanner to suggest getting back to work.

"But not you Charles. I need you to come with me to town. There's a shipment of supplies that has come for us that cannot sit around the docks all night."

131

 August 12 — 11:07 p.m.

Okay, it's late and I need to wake up early for work again tomorrow so I'm just going to jump into it and cover my reactions at the end.

After I was sure the Tanners left the house I slowly snuck my way upstairs. Even with no one in the house, it felt like I needed to be quiet with my footsteps. I made my way to the junction in the hallways on the upper story using a flashlight so as to not broadcast my snooping with unauthorized lights on.

My aim was to explore the rooms Charlie had brushed past when he gave me the tour earlier. Putting caution to the wind, I stepped into the first room as quickly as possible and scanned the room with my flashlight.

Fossils and antiques it looked like. Nothing too out of the ordinary for this house. Not thinking I had much time to snoop, I hastily moved to the next room across the hall.

More fossils, but something caught my eye as I was leaving. It was a picture of a young man and a pretty young woman with two beauty marks. What stopped me was that the man looked a bit like Charlie. It had to have been Mr. Tanner when he was younger.

Oh gosh does that mean I already know what Charlie's going to look like at that age?

Erm, anyway. It was possible the young lady was Charlie's grandmother, she did kind of have his smile anyway. Why had I never heard anything about her? What happened to her, and what about pictures of Charlie's parents?

Either way, besides having way too many storage rooms for the old and dead there didn't seem to be much for me on the second floor. As I left the room I wearily glanced down the darkened hallway that would lead to Charlie and Mr. Tanner's room. There was a good chance anything that I could be looking for might be in their rooms, but I didn't think it would be smart to chance it. The awkwardness that would follow being caught in their bedrooms just simply was not worth it.

With that in mind, I figured the downstairs would be my next target. Maybe there was something in Mr. Tanner's study. Then I thought about the strange lights I had seen when I was sneaking around the outside of their house and almost met a gruesome forest creature end.

Having something in my sight, I tiptoed back down to the entryway to the staircase and spiraled down. The few and far between windows didn't offer much ambient light from outside, as the blinds had been drawn. The only light in the house was coming from the kitchen and the mailroom, where I was supposed to be working. My night was beginning to feel like a bad horror movie as I moved, flashlight in hand, towards the more sketchy, darker rooms in the house.

I intended to stop at Mr. Tanner's study, but my curiosity over the rooms I'd never been in won out and I entered the next room over.

I was a bit shocked to see what appeared to be a normal family room. A few couches, a TV, what looked like a laptop over on a desk. Not entirely tidy, but comfy. I felt better knowing that Charlie had some connection to the outside world. Though I was wondering at that point if this had to been the room where I saw all those strange lights.

By then I had to have been snooping around for near 20 minutes, and I was seriously starting to think I should just get back to work. There didn't seem to be anything out of the ordinary– for the Tanners– and I had probably just found the source of some of my queries. It didn't make sense to keep going.

But then something caught my eye– a doorknob. It looked different than all the others, old and bronze with an intricate handle. I stood in the hallway for a good two minutes grumbling and starting for the door, before turning around and faking towards the mailroom before yet again turning back to the door.

My flashlight reflected off of a small portrait on the wall next to the door, darkened with time. I had to get up close and personal with the wall to see it properly even with the help of my flashlight.

I felt a cold chill go down my spine.

It was old, obviously very old. The paint was curling and cracked in such a way, not to mention the discoloring of the paper itself, to an art aficionado like myself it was apparent it was the real deal.

But it was the same woman I had just seen upstairs in the photo with the younger Mr. Tanner. I had my face up against the glass practically to take in all the details. The hair, the face shape, the eyes, everything. She even had the same two little beauty marks on her cheek that the other did, in the same exact spots.

So why was this woman in a 1950s photo, also in this painting from over *100* years ago?

I shook my head like I had water in my ears, before taking a few good-sized steps backwards. I was being stupid right?

It was just a coincidence.

And then I heard the unmistakable squeak of the back door, and without thinking bolted into the room next to the mysterious woman's portrait. I backed up until I bumped into a table, stifling a yelp and turned off my flashlight. I crouched down next to the table and watched for footsteps by the door.

It seemed like an eternity. Besides the footfall, my own breathing was the only thing I could hear in the silence.

Then, I saw the shadow under the door. But it passed, and then came back… before going back down the hallway and what I believed to be the sounds of someone going back outside.

Panic ripped through me when I realized that the Tanners were home.

If I was screwed, there was no point really hiding myself. If the Tanners knew I was somewhere else in their home, why continue with the ninja act?

So standing up, I used the light of my flashlight to find the light switch on the wall.

I had a mild heart attack when I turned back around to view the room.

It looked like a freaking war room. There were maps ALL over the walls, and spread over tables. The maps looked like they covered all stages of map-making, from the oldest, hand drawn European and Asian style, to the maps on the tables that looked like satellite imaging.

They were all marked, either with yarn or string, or on some of the newer ones with marker.

When I walked up to get a closer look at some of the older maps, I realized one was in Greek and covered most of the Mediterranean. Now, I wasn't actually the greatest history student in class, but I was certain most of the countries on the map were long gone. Macedonia, Lydia, Carthage... okay, that last one rings a bell for some reason.

I moved on to the maps of Asia, and though my geography wasn't the best, I was pretty sure that what was labeled as *Terra Incognita* was actually eastern Russia.

Getting close enough to view the maps, I noticed that next to me were rows of old journals in a bookshelf. In fact, there were so many journals, they filled the entire very large bookshelf. I decided to look through a couple, and tip-toed to reach one of the many piled up on top, not wanting disturb the bookshelf itself.

I groaned at the age of the one picked up, feeling suddenly like I was sullying a piece of history. I gingerly opened the front cover and looked at the name inscribed inside.

Ignatius L. Tanner. 1750.

Yep, I probably ruined what was an ancient and precious piece of family history. Well, since it was already open it didn't really matter if I looked at a few more pages right? That's what I figured, and ignore the guilt weighing me down inside.

I felt a bit less guilty when I saw that the journal was half drawings. Suddenly it was relevant to my work! Flipping through the pages was a real treat, honestly. The art was beautifully done, and the handwriting was amazing.

Almost illegible it was so fancy, but amazing.

Soon though, three quarters the way through the writing stopped. I won't lie and say I wasn't disappointed, so I flipped back to the last page of writing. There was artwork of a dinosaur on one side, and writing on the other.

I **knew** that dinosaur. It was one of the few I ever looked up. A *Velociraptor*. Back when Charlie made his joking comment about the scar on his leg, I was a bit in the dark. So when we got back from camping I looked up the thing just to see.

You know, I'm pretty sure they said the first ever discovered *Velociraptor* skeleton was in the 1920s. So why was Charlie's great-times-20-grandpappy drawing one perfectly? In the *1700s*.

I looked at it a bit closer and noticed a few feathers on the underside of the arms. How on earth did Ignatius Tanner know about feathers on dinosaurs?

I tried looking for any signs that the picture had been tampered with, maybe altered more recently, but I couldn't find any. That wasn't to say it wasn't, I just couldn't find any smoking guns. Along with the small inscription detailing the animal without giving a proper name to it, it looked like Ignatius had actually seen the creature.

But that was crazy, I told myself, trying to ignore that voice in the back of my head that was saying no matter how much sense I tried to make out of this situation there wasn't any to be made.

It was weird, everything about it was weird, and the more journals I flipped through, the weirder it got. More depictions of things none of these people should have ever seen. Not all of the individuals were named Tanner, but it seemed likely that they were related somehow. I saw at least one name that read *Marie nee Tanner Roberts* that seemed to support my idea.

Forgetting that the Tanners were probably wondering where I was, I decided to look through more of the room. On the opposite wall there were many papers posted, often times over parts of maps.

I had barely gotten up to read them when I felt a puff of breath on my neck.

I, understandably, freaked the hell out. My survival instincts kicked in, and I brought my elbow back into whoever was behind me. As soon as I hit a warm body I knew I just did something amazingly stupid.

"OW, what the… what. Ow! Eliza that ***hurt!***"

"Chuck?! What, is the sneaking up on people thing genetic?!" I was startled and kind of pushing the blame towards him.

He gave me a look like, *are you serious?* While clutching his stomach with one hand.

"What are you even doing in here? Are you *snooping* on us?!" He straightened his position and had the decency to look a bit appalled.

"I– I wouldn't be if you… didn't have snoop… worthy… stuff." I finished lamely, waving my hands around. Charlie had his judging you silently face on. "Are you a *vampire?!*"

Charlie's eyes widened for a half a second, and I could see the wheels in his head turning as though what I had just said took extra juice to process.

And then he doubled over laughing.

"That's what you come up with? My family's a bit off so I must be a vampire? Don't you think my vampire-powers would have prevented me from taking your boney elbow to the ribs? Not to mention *vampires are fictional.*"

Okay, let's be clear, I didn't actually think he was a vampire. I've just seen one too many bad movies.

Moving on.

"Fine then, how do you explain that woman's portrait or… or all of those field journals!?" I pointed the accusing finger at him, and he sent back a mildly befuddled expression.

"Who? Grandma Violet? What about her?"

"That picture is over a hundred years old, Chuck! And those journals, the things in them don't match their time period!"

He shifted uncomfortably, and shrugged his shoulders and made an, "Oh..." noise.

I knew there was no chance of him telling me anything straight out. It felt a bit like being betrayed, and I didn't know why. It's not like we were officially dating. Or even officially friends.

Still it sucked though.

"Let's get back to work," I said "Can you just..." I sighed heavily, "not tell your grandfather I was here?"

Charlie ran a hand through his already messy hair, and nodded.

"Will you not come back here?" he asked.

"To this room, or to your house?"

He looked a bit pained for a moment, like he was seriously weighing all options.

"To this room."

I nodded. I went to move past him, but as I left the room I noticed something he was standing just in front of. A map on one of the tables.

It was a map of Northwestern Washington. There was a large area circled in red just off the coastline of Orcas Island and a little note next to it. In motion, it was hard to read it, but all I needed to see was one date.

August 20th. I cast one glance back at Charlie who was looking at some of the things on the wall, stone faced and glum.

Just what were they planning?

August 13 — 8:31 p.m.

This whole overtime experience has been… Annoying? Slow? Aggravating? Stagnant?

It feels like the last few days Charlie and I had begun butting heads. I guess maybe it was okay that we were work friends and pleasant enough to one another in those regards, but as soon as anything borderline romantic arose every other little problem popped its nasty little head out too. We're starting to get into little tiffs every few minutes, nipping at each other's heels.

It didn't help that I didn't get much sleep last night. I could barely keep my eyes closed after thinking about everything that was happening, and what I still didn't know. Judging from the bags under his eyes, Charlie was probably thinking similar things.

I still really like Charlie, but two teens playing Spy vs Spy, or some sort of weird passive aggressive game of chicken won't end well. I can't even count the number of times today that Mr. Tanner asked one or the other of us to go run some little task for him just to separate our bickering.

Charlie would get upset with my attitude, and I'd get upset at him for being upset with me, and so on.

There were never any huge fights, just exasperated noises, heavy sighs, raised tones and clenched fists. Occasionally he'd give me these pointed looks, then glance at his grandfather, as if to say "You don't understand, I can't tell you because it's my *family*." **Whatever, Chuck.**

Charlie's subtle looks are a bit unrefined, but I suppose that's understandable given he's barely around normal humans.

It seems odd to think we were cuddling on the camping trip less than a week ago. What felt like the beginning of some sort of spring fling, summer love type journal has turned into… whatever *this* is.

Nothing good that's for sure. Right now it's looking like I'll be going home with bad blood towards my uncle, and a relationship I don't know if I ever want to tell my friends back home in California about.

I'm certain now that I can't come back here, that any dreams of college here would be stupid. I'll just go to some school near by in Irvine and try and forget anything ever happened on Orcas Island.

Though as of tonight, there wasn't much needing forgetting. My earlier dreams of an overtime snooping-fest were short lived. When I arrived at work today I found that stupid Harlequin painting in the entry hall. Didn't take too much brain power to figure out it was Charlie sending a warning. A spangled, checkered, masked creepy man, but a warning nonetheless.

Not that it stopped me of course, but when I went on a bathroom break with a mind of going to the same room I saw last night, I found Charlie lounging against the door.

"Little far from our powder room, huh?" He smirked, and it was pretty obvious he had spent some time thinking up a quip.

Smiling back at him, I handed him an old journal. Ignatius Tanner's old journal to be precise.

"Oh I was just returning this, but I'm glad you're here so you could do it for me instead." Charlie looked a bit surprised at the item resting in his hand and shot me with an incredulous expression.

"When did you—" his eyes narrowed as it dawned on him, "– when you took a bathroom break last night, right? You snuck back in here and lifted it."

It was true, I hadn't had time to do much else last night, but I wanted to read the journal more in depth. So earlier I made an excuse and grabbed the journal, and only the journal. If I grabbed more than one, Charlie would notice them missing if he checked in the room again.

But, knowing my TV-drama lawyer logic, I just smiled and said, "I don't have any recollection of that event."

He sighed, and ran a hand over his face.

"Eliza, do you not get that I don't want you knowing about this stuff?"

"Do you get that I don't particularly care? And what's this about not wanting me to know? Before you **wanted** to tell me, but you couldn't." I shot back at him.

"It's not like that— I do wish I could tell you about it. But you can't, and it's not your secret to know." He took a shaky breath, and locked eyes with me, "And... are you really sure you don't kind of already know?"

"I have plenty of ideas, but I'm trying to rule out the really crazy ones first," I said.

Charlie smiled, though a bit hollowly, "What, like vampires?"

"Something like that Charlie." I said firmly, before turning back around to head down the hallway.

"You called me Charlie." I paused and turned back around.

"Sorry?"

"No, I mean... you've been calling me Chuck since yesterday. It's like your way of saying *I'm angry with you so much that I don't deem your name speakable*." He looked a bit happier than he had since the camping trip.

I smiled, "*Let's get back to work*, Charles." and made my way back to the staircase, and didn't turn around when he called out a weak, "Hey!"

It was a lighter moment between us, but he was still keeping things from me. Maybe even rightfully so, but I couldn't stop now. Not that I had gotten so far. What I had read in Ignatius' journal didn't help to quell my interests either. The ancient Tanner didn't write anything specific, and made a good point to skirt around the exact truth. However, it was obvious, that even as far back as the 1700s the Tanner's had been a remarkably strange clan.

I managed to spend all of Saturday evening and Sunday completely depressed. The unfortunate, can't-tell-anyone-why kind of depressed culminating from knowing too damn much. It most certainly didn't help being around Pat, who's been his usual chipper self.

Sometimes Pat will just ignore me, like a petulant child or a teenage girl giving me the silent treatment. Other times he'll lecture me about "my future," or the Tanners. Auntie doesn't say anything, and you can tell it's because she's stressed out, too. She's probably gotten to the point where the sounds of Pat and I arguing are just white noise.

I really don't want to spend my last few weeks on Orcas Island stressed out— my neck can't take it! Speaking of the Tanners, what am I supposed to do there? Today has been alright I guess, me and Charlie aren't bickering like we had been last week. Not as much anyway. But sometimes I still want to rip out my hair and stuff it in his mouth to get him to shut the hell up.

 And what am I supposed to do about Pat? I'm pretty sure we're well beyond the point of making nice with each other and having all of our problems magically fix themselves like in some cartoon.

Okay, maybe I could get over some things if he'd apologize to me, but I don't think that's very likely.

I'm sure at a time like this my mother would say something like, "You should take the high road and apologize first!"

To which I would say, "I have nothing to apologize for. I said I was sorry for sneaking out that night! I've been an angel since!" Minus the snooping around the Tanner house thing.

My father would probably say to her, "Patrick's been as stubborn as a rock as long as I've known him. Which has been… always. Just let the titans clash." Which would be easy for him to say, since he's not the one dealing with him right now. I mean, he's in Tampa!

They can swing on over to a theme park, letting me suffer while blaming it on conflicting personalities!

I'm getting pissed off over something I thought my father *might* say?

See, this is exactly why I need a break. Maybe this weekend I'll ask Auntie if she wants to go do fun girl things around the island. That way I can take my mind off of Pat and Charlie… In theory of course, because she'll probably bring it up anyway.

Okay, I really need to go take a long bath or something to relax. I'm not sure if I'll be able to just turn my brain off, but at the least hot water might relax my neck some. If nothing else I can wash off the layer of dirt I obtained at work today while helping Charlie organize Cambrian-era fossils.

Right. Night, Journal.

Tonight is the big night. It coincides with what Ignatius' journal said, something about the seventh day of the growing crescent moon.

It feels like this is the night everything has been leading up to.

The week up until this point has been pretty boring. We've been going back through specific time periods and working on fossils. Some I'm used to, some I hadn't seen or heard of before.

On Monday, like my last entry said, we were working on the Cambrian era with some of the earliest fish. Charlie told me fish were pretty rare, and for a long time they were believed to have evolved during the Ordovician rather than Late Cambrian.

Tuesday was Ordovician, studying some of my new favorite creatures—the family of Nautiloids. They're cephalopods from phylum Mollusca, but they're undeniably interesting. They're very strange creatures. You might recognize the living example: the nautilus. They originated earlier than the Ordovician but didn't flourish until the Ordovician.

Wednesday was the short Silurian age, with a collection of the more

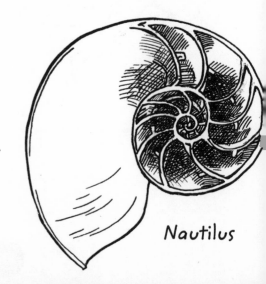

Nautilus

well-known trilobites and the less well-known (but perfectly horrifying) eurypterid. Eurypterids are essentially gargantuan sea scorpions. They weren't actually scorpions, but the thought still gives me goose bumps.

Thursday was the Devonian. One of the major fossil remains we looked at is *Drepanaspis gemuendenensis*, an odd, early fish-like creature without a jaw.

Friday was the Carboniferous period, which had a wide variety of flora and fauna. We had our work cut out for us looking through everything. Charlie liked teasing me by showing me giant fossilized insects. The worst was *Megarachne servinei*, a species of eurypterid that looked like a cat-sized spider. Certainly not something that would be killed with the swift heel of a heavy boot.

It's not long now before I go back home to Irvine. I was under the impression that Mr. Tanner was covering as much, on a general broad basis, information as possible. Maybe he was even trying to drown me in work in hopes that I'd loose some steam. It was pretty obvious he knew I knew... something.

Technically I'm not even sure I know what that something is.

Here's to hoping I find out tonight?

I'm going to be following the Tanners out to the island that was circled on the map in their home; Matia Island. I needed a reason to go out, so I used a convenient excuse, "Uh. My friend Alex and I. We're having a girls night out."

I did actually see Alex briefly, but it was more her accidentally running into me while I was wolfing down some fast food. We talked for a moment before she left. It struck me as odd that for someone I'm using as an alibi, I didn't know much about her.

She's nice, as always. It still kind of annoys me.

Anyway, now I'm at the docks. Which is probably a really stupid place to be for a teenage girl by herself. I had not worked out how I was going to get the two and a half miles from Orcas Island to Matia Island. I guess I thought I would hitch a ride or something. I hadn't really thought this one through all the way but now that I'm here at the docks I see what I'm going to do.

I'm going to do something crazy. I'm going to kayak to Matia. There's a kayak here, and a paddle too, and they are not locked up. Island people sure are trusting. I'm glad I went canoeing with Charlie, so at least I sort of know what I'm doing.

I'm going to bring you along, Journal, obviously. If something happens—I mean, I need to record everything I can.

9:35 p.m.

Well, Pat, if you ever read this journal entry you may think I'm a liar or a crazy teenager making stuff up for fun. I'm not even sure what I believe anymore except that I better use the time I have to keep track of what's happening. So starting where I left off before:

The light was fading fast, and even though the waters were calm enough that I didn't feel sick, the encroaching darkness was more than a little disturbing. That and kayaking is hard work! Really, really hard work. I'm surprised I'm not dead, or in the belly of some whale.

With the setting sun and then the waxing moon to guide me, I finally reached Matia. It took a while to get there. A long, scary heart-beating while. It was well past dark by the time I reached the island. My destination was a rocky cove on the northern side of the island. However, it was apparently NOT the Tanner's destination. They must have gone to the north face of the island where I was certain there were no docks, just sharp jagged slippery rocks. I didn't know what to do at that point, as my arms were exhausted and the trip was pretty scary.

My heart sank as I realized I'd either be kayaking back in the dark around wave slapped jagged rocks or I would end up walking through a dark forest with no idea where I was supposed to be going.

I was honestly ready to call it a night and just camp out. I wasn't even sure where the Tanners might be on the island.

I certainly didn't think my plan through enough. Kayaking back at this point seemed crazy. I was tired, the waves were picking up and the darkness of the

night made the two and a half mile trip back seem even more daunting, if not stupid or impossible.

Which meant I was stranded on Matia Island *unless* I found the Tanners. Talk about bad luck.

I decided to hoof it and try my luck in finding the Tanners. The only saving grace about stomping through Matia's National Forest with little but a flashlight to guide me was the paths. Being a common hiking destination, there were plenty of paths scattered about the island. The black lining on that saving grace was that the paths only extended for just over a mile, and didn't cover the entire island.

My walk was peaceful enough, nevermind the occasional owl's hoot or animals skittering along in the underbrush. Normally I would have been freaked out, hearing something moving around out of sight, but Matia was small and isolated and I didn't think any pumas would be leaping out of the dark and going for my throat.

Walking alone like that gets a person thinking. Not that there was much else to do, really, with sightseeing not an option at night. No one to talk to, no one to joke with. It'd get pretty lonely, if you couldn't retreat back into your mind.

Why was I hired at all? I mean, this is something I probably should have asked Charlie… I suppose I just had other things on my mind at the time. Was hiring an illustrator instead of a photographer a way of avoiding photographic evidence like I suspected?

When I came to the end of the trail, my thoughts were broken. There was a small, animal type path going out into the deep woods, but it didn't look all that inviting. Not to mention, being in an area where there could be drop-offs, steep slopes or even a crevasse. Walking out into that would be foolish at the least, and at the most potentially deadly.

But somewhere out in the between the branches I heard a voice. A masculine voice, then, for a moment I swore I saw a flashlight's ray. It had to be the Tanners—my mind buzzing, I pushed out into the woods and ignored the feeling of spider webs against my arms and face. Brushing them away only with an absent mind. They were close, and moreover they were my ride home, and with sticks and lord knows what else in my hair that was the more important issue.

I almost broke through the tree line, but stopped just before. My entire reason for being out here was to find out what they were up to, wasn't it? This was a perfect chance, so I stuck my head out just far enough to see Charlie and Mr. Tanner moving about in an open patch in the surrounding forest.

Even though the moon wasn't super big, its light made everything seem brighter. The treetops had a glow about them and the long grass was swaying. There wasn't a single manmade sound.

"Just about time, now. All items ready and checked, Charles?" Mr. Tanner said, his voice sounding louder than it ever had before.

Charlie replied with a very strong, "Yes, sir. All set. All equipment checked, ready to depart." I smiled in my hiding spot. Charlie had a very formal attitude when it came to showtime. Though I wasn't sure what "showtime" was yet.

I didn't know what I was waiting for, but for some reason I felt like I'd know when it was time to reveal myself.

"Ready?"

And that was it.

I pushed through a small wild berry bush, and winced when I felt a bramble stick my arm. I stumbled on a tree root, but still neither of the Tanners noticed me as they faced the other direction. I reached for Charlie's jacket to sturdy myself, and hesitantly said, "Charlie," around the same time they both turned. They looked immediately startled, and Charlie called back a very bewildered,

"Eliza?! What are yo—"

And that was the last thing I heard before a burst of orange light blinded me. I looked down at my outstretched hand. I was grabbing for something that was no longer there.

Charlie and Mr. Tanner vanished before my very eyes. They were gone.

I bit my lip and raised my flashlight in front of me. There wasn't trace of anyone, but the long grass was slightly trampled from where Charlie and Mr. Tanner had stood.

I'd been left behind.

I noticed tracks leading to the spot they had been standing, and while there were none moving away from the spot they had been, I decided after a few fretful moments to follow the tracks. What I found was their ship bobbing in the water, in a small natural inlet of the island. The boat was still tied up in the inlet, which meant they hadn't left that way and I still had a way back to the main island. After almost slipping on at least five algae-covered rocks, I hobbled my way into the boat and found a powerful LED flashlight. Deciding to trade it for mine and relieved to have a better light source, I made my way back onto land.

I trudged back through the forest to the spot they left from. My cell phone didn't get service out here, but I saw five missed calls from Auntie and Pat's home phone number. I suppose "girls night out" was lasting a bit long… I'm so going to be in trouble when I get home.

"Well, this sucks," I said to myself, and sat down in the grass. I've been sitting here, writing in you by the light of the flashlight, for, oh… nearly an hour now. Definitely a bummer.

I could totally go the rest of my life without being stuck on an island in the middle of the night all alone. It wouldn't be so bad if I knew when they'd be back. Or if I had packed a book or my drawing supplies.

It's a beautiful night out. It would make a great picture. Wait! I **do** have a camera.

I just took a picture with my cell phone's camera. It's not the best picture in the world, but the moon looks amazing over the treetops.

They're back.

Once again I'm writing on a boat. Hopefully it doesn't make me queasy like last time. We circled around the island and retrieved the kayak.

A bright light (red this time) announced their return. My phone and journal toppled into the grass because I stood up so fast. Mr. Tanner asked how long they'd been gone, and I clung to Charlie like a little kid grabbing on to the middle of the spinning teacup ride at Disneyland. It took a second for me to realize Mr. Tanner had said anything at all, and for a minute I wanted to hug him as well. Then I figured he wouldn't appreciate human contact very much.

They'd been gone just over an hour. He nodded knowingly.

I turned back to Charlie.

"*Now* are you going to tell me what the hell is going on?"

"I'm really sorry about keeping this from you, but it's just… *you know*."

I shook my head. I didn't care. Not really. Mr. Tanner vanished, and before I could ask where he'd gone, Charlie handed me a flower. I took it delicately into my hand.

"*Sagaria cilentana*… Cretaceous period. They're extinct now. I really am sorry, Eliza."

Let me reiterate that for you; *Cretaceous* period. Yeah.

"So… you are– you're… what exactly?" I asked hollowly, feeling a bit light in the head.

"I guess the general term would be *time travelers*,?" Charlie said, with a quick shrug of his shoulders. He had a dusting of rain on him, and considering it hadn't rained in quite some time, it was completely odd.

I shook my head from side to side, "No, no. Time travel doesn't exist. It can't exist. That's just a sci-fi plot device for weird British television series."

Unfortunately, it made more sense than anything else I could come up with considering the circumstances. The skeletons, the animal corpses, the journals– all of it would make sense in a time-travelling scenario.

"Why do you think I didn't tell you? Because it does sound insane. All of it sounds insane!" Charlie huffed.

"Fine then, how does it work? Why here? Why tonight?" I responded.

"It's complicated."

I gave him my best evil eye.

"Okay, fine. It's a genetic predisposition. That's why my grandfather and I, as well as my ancestors, could make leaps. And as for why here and why tonight, it's because of the energy flows of the earth, the moon, and water. Our bodies are affected by the moon's pull, the different pulses of electromagnetic energy along ley lines and the movement of water. These things affect us and our ability to travel. They tend to change fairly frequently, so the times and places that we can leap from vary."

I kept quiet while he was explaining, but I was back to none of it making much sense. What did genetics have to do with energy, and I thought ley lines were just something invented to get gullible people to buy things they didn't need. I apparently didn't have to say anything, because Charlie noticed my incredulous expression.

"My family has been studying this phenomenon since the 1700s and we still don't understand much except that there is an energy grid to the planet and certain places at certain times are more turned on than others. Grandpa and I spend a lot of time tracking possible jump-off points, and we're not always correct. Sometimes we don't leave the present. And most of the time we have no idea where we are going to time travel to, except that it is usually to the very distant past. We've had little to do with human history."

I wasn't sure I believed him. He looked so earnest and vulnerable though. And there was the undeniable fact he and his grandfather had just disappeared in front of my eyes. And then reappeared.

I'm pretty sure that even if it had been an elaborate magic trick, they wouldn't have done it in the middle-of-nowhere-Washington at night.

So I shut him up with a kiss. The impact of the flower had hit me. It was the most romantic gift of flowers in the history of time, and I know my history by now.

I've been out for hours by now, and my premise of just going out with a friend won't hold up. I know I'll get questioned like a CIA informant when I get home, but I really don't care right now. My mind is racing, and my heart's pounding and there's no way I'd be able to wrap my head around any of this.

I'm sure I'll sit bolt upright in my bed in the morning unable to rid myself of question, but for now, I'm content.

Maybe I didn't really need to know their secret, maybe it was just the challenge of finding out. I needed to feel like a hero, at a time when I couldn't even convince my own uncle I wasn't a felon-to-be.

I'm on a boat ride with my—dare I say—boyfriend on a beautiful night, with a beautiful flower.

I'm in a place I love, with people I love.

I couldn't be happier.

Well, maybe if Mr. Tanner wasn't here, too.

Last night was an ordeal. I mean after the time traveling and prehistoric flowers in the middle of the night.

I got home near midnight. I hadn't answered my cell phone all night, so when I finally got home I was met with a couple of unhappy faces.

I said I was going to dinner with Alex, and I ended up running into the Tanners while out. **Completely** truthful.

It was, however, hard for them not to notice our clothes looked worse for wear (especially Charlie, whose jeans were still damp from mooring and unmooring the motorboat). I was windblown and cold, with a small grass stain on my rear from where I'd been sitting on the ground. Unfortunately, Mr. Tanner looked almost untouched.

This all added up to us arriving A: in the middle of the night, B: looking like we had been traipsing through a swamp, and C: without having answered my phone.

I was racking my brain trying to think of something, anything, to say but I didn't have to worry about it. Auntie said, "We'd have been worried sick if Mr. Tanner hadn't called us!"

This caused my head to snap in Mr. Tanner's direction, giving him a *you-did-what?* look. I flashed back to when Mr. Tanner had gone to load supplies into the boat while Charlie and I—got caught up in one another.

Mr. Tanner had a cool and calm expression. While my uncle was the grumpy-with-a-heart-of-gold type, Mr. Tanner was a poker-faced gentleman. He had vouched for me.

Truthfully, I wanted to tell Auntie and Pat what actually happened... or at least Auntie, but it wasn't my secret to tell. They'd let me into their world under the assumption I was reliable and trustworthy.

Mr. Tanner looked at Pat. "We took a boat out to Matia Island to observe the moon and wildlife. The miss Alexandra couldn't make it however. I'm sorry my grandson looks so disheveled, he moored the boat for us." He was as good of a not-liar as I was. He'd make a good politician.

That seemed to mend some bridges that would have otherwise been burning piles of rubble.

Auntie asked how well I was working with them. She glanced at Pat from the corner of her eye, and I could tell this was more about him than any urge she really felt to ask about my work.

Mr. Tanner must have felt some of the heat from Pat's laser eye. He said, "She's a very capable worker. She takes very few breaks and concentrates on the task at hand. You should be pleased. If you'd like I can send you copies of some of her work."

A ripple of surprise ran over Pat's face before it crumbled back into its usual state of ire. Auntie said that would be nice, and she'd fax copies to my mom and dad. People still use fax machines?

"That's a pretty flower, Eliza. Did you pick it on Matia? I don't think I've ever seen one like it before..."

I froze, and opened and closed my mouth like a carp before Charlie responded with, "We have a garden. It's a foreign species. The name escapes me..."

My eyes narrowed at that. Lord knows Charles Augustus Tanner would never forget the scientific name of a plant species. But he'd picked me flowers. Prehistoric flowers. I was holding a living fossil, and it sure beat the hell out of *Anomalocaris*. I felt like grinning stupidly at everything and nothing.

Then suddenly the world stopped turning. The fabric of the space-time continuum was ripped to bits—Mr. Tanner invited Pat fishing. Tomorrow morning.

That can't possibly go well, I thought.

Then everyone said good night. I really, really needed sleep, but a shower was in order first.

Sleep didn't come as easily as I would have thought. In the moment I just accepted what Charlie told me. While lying down in bed, I began thinking. That little voice that says, "are you sure about that?" kept chiming in no matter what plausible explanation I could come up with. On the flip side, whenever I simply tried denying anything he said, the same voice would chime in with, "but what if it's true?"

All in all, it was a fretful night, but I did manage to fall asleep after a few hours.

When I woke up this morning to the smell of freshly cooked—you know, I was so hungry I don't actually remember—I inhaled it. Auntie informed me Pat was out fishing with Mr. Tanner. I was shocked.

"He didn't take a baseball bat with him, did he?" I muttered.

Auntie looked at me, confused. "Why would they need a baseball bat?"

Clubbing someone's head in. Clubbing sea life. Threatening young'uns and their ways.

"I dunno," I responded.

The rest of the day was spent with little activity. Auntie and I talked, took a walk… she even helped me with my flower. Since it was picked rather than uprooted, she suggested I press it and save it between two sheets of glass. (Lord knows if it would even survive a pot, since its few-million-year-old natural environment was long gone. That is, if what Charlie told me was true…)

I'm sure Auntie knew me and Charlie's relationship wasn't that of just coworkers, but I'm glad she didn't say anything about it, except for a quick, "that Charles seems like a nice boy."

What do you say to that? I just nodded. I was thinking of ways to change the subject, but Auntie didn't continue the conversation beyond that point.

The rest of my Sunday was quiet and relaxed until 5:00 when Pat got home. The hairs on the back of my neck stood up when he called me outside. What had they talked about? Had Mr. Tanner eased the situation or aggravated it?

I gave Auntie a if-I'm-not-back-in-ten-minutes-get-help look and padded outside onto the porch. Pat was leaning against the house cleaning his fishing equipment. We stood in silence. I was getting antsy.

"That Tanner. Not a bad man. Caught a three-footer."

I blinked. Had he really just complimented Mr. Tanner?

"I still don't trust his grandson. Boys at that age... just armpit hair and hormones."

Well—I—okay?

"Orville said you do good work. Wants to have you back next summer."

I hadn't heard *that* before. You'd think that would have come up at some point last night.

"You're more than welcome to stay here again, so you can work for him."

I nodded stiffly and said thank you before heading inside. Pat said after me, "Before you leave for home, we're all going fishing again. Tanners, too."

"Okay." I went back inside. ***What just happened***, was the only thing going through my mind.

I don't think everything between us has been smoothed over, but that is probably as close as Pat will get to saying, "I'm sorry for being a paranoid dweeb. Please forgive me and grace us with your presence of awesomeness next year as well."

It's not a perfect ending, but I guess it's good enough.

Anyway, time for dinner.

Night, Journal.

I know I didn't write anything last week, and now I'm realizing that wasn't the best idea on the planet. I won't deny the fact that it's been hard for me to wrap my head around the place I find myself in. Not the physical location, of course, but the idea of Charlie's situation. That now I've somehow wrapped myself all up, because I was the one who couldn't let the mystery go.

Most days I just ignore the looming weirdness that is the time travel issue. On the best days I just accept it and move on, and on the worst days I'll lie in bed and won't be able to sleep because my mind won't stop racing.

Thankfully while at work, new projects been preventing me from thinking too deeply about my own problems.

I only have a very short period of time before I go home. Less than a week actually, on Monday, which means I've been busy. Mr. Tanner seemed to realize my time was short as well and decided to make the most of it. I've been working my ass off all week.

Of course, Auntie wanted to squeeze in as much "family time" as she possibly could, so from the moment I got home from work to the moment I went to bed, Auntie was wanting to do something.

Then there's Charlie, who similarly had a moment of holy-crap-she's-only-going-to-be-here-for-another-week, so we went out on a few dates. Well, we went out to dinner and took a couple walks… I'm not sure if that constitutes a real date or not, but it was nice. A change of pace from the earlier weeks when we had been off-and-on fighting and bickering. Since Matia we've become closer than we had before. We've been talking more openly about our lives before this summer, and about our families.

I'm not sure why he felt he wasn't getting sufficient Eliza time at work, where I saw him for eight hours a day, but he said it was different when we were just out on the town. I probably would've agreed if every moment of my time hadn't been spent doing **something** like it was those last few days.

I think Uncle Pat started to realize he hadn't spent much time with me either, given our—I think "tiff" is too light a phrase, but "war" would be a bit over the top. So in his own way, he was trying to reconnect.

There just weren't enough hours in a day to fit everything in. It was exhausting and exhilarating at the same time.

The project I was working on at the Tanners' (which had turned me into a zombie, but with better hair) was the *Maiacetus* skeleton. Remember the *Maiacetus* skull I mentioned way back when? Big thing with way too many teeth? Well, when I got to work on Monday, Mr. Tanner gave me back the illustrations I'd drawn of it. At first I was thinking, *Oh no, he must have hated my work*, but as it turns out, he wanted me to draw the ENTIRE skeleton. And then, to top it all off, we would be constructing a model of it. *To scale*.

So, for Monday and part of Tuesday, I drew like a fiend, a possessed soul whose only mission was to accurately illustrate this ancient monstrosity. And it had nothing to do with wanting to ignore other giant elephants in the room, like say time travel.

On Tuesday we started to assemble the outline of the skeletal structure. Marking where everything was supposed to go in wire on the skull was simple enough since I'd already drawn the *real* skull, but the rest of the skeleton was a bit more difficult. I needed textbooks to get an accurate account of the detail.

By the end of Wednesday we'd plotted everything to scale and accounted for the many, many bones the thing had. *Maiacetus inuus*, much like many four-legged animals (though it was on land very rarely), had a number of vertebrae and an extra long tail that was difficult when dealing with the number of bones and size of vertebrae. There were so many little bones, and if you didn't get them just right and in the correct position you end up with a dolphin hippo monster with a bent tail. Needless to say there were a few stress related tantrums at the end of the week. Thankfully, Mr. Tanner was overseeing most of the work. He has slightly more knowledge than Charlie when it comes to forensic animal physiology.

Charlie collected materials like plaster and steel for the project, which we used on Thursday and part of Friday. The real difficulty was getting everything where it needed to be, skeletal-wise. The reconstruction was actually fairly simple and pretty fun. It took a while of course (it ate up a good portion of two days), but it was far more enjoyable and much less stressful than, say, mapping EXACTLY where each SPECIFIC tooth went in the jaw.

By the end of today (Friday), we finally got to the best part of the project: painting it. It was by no means a clean and tidy job, but it was fun as hell. We used shellac to give the fake bones a fossilized look. After four hours painting, the fake creature was complete. Charlie and I collapsed. The room was large enough we could safely flop onto the floor without getting shellac all over our pants.

Then Mr. Tanner came in and told us the Burke people would be here the following week to pick it up.

"Burke? Like, The Burke Museum?" I asked.

Yes, *that* Burke. Something I worked on is going to be displayed in the Burke Museum. The Burke has some world-class exhibits, some of the best. Their primary focus is on the Pacific Northwest, so they cover everything from native tribes of the area to prehistoric fossils. It's one of the more famous tourist spots in Seattle.

Most of my last week on Orcas Island was eaten up by that project. I can't say I'm bummed about it (I mean, it's the *Burke*), but this means I'll be trying to fit in as much time with everyone as I can before I go home.

Anyway. Good night, Journal.

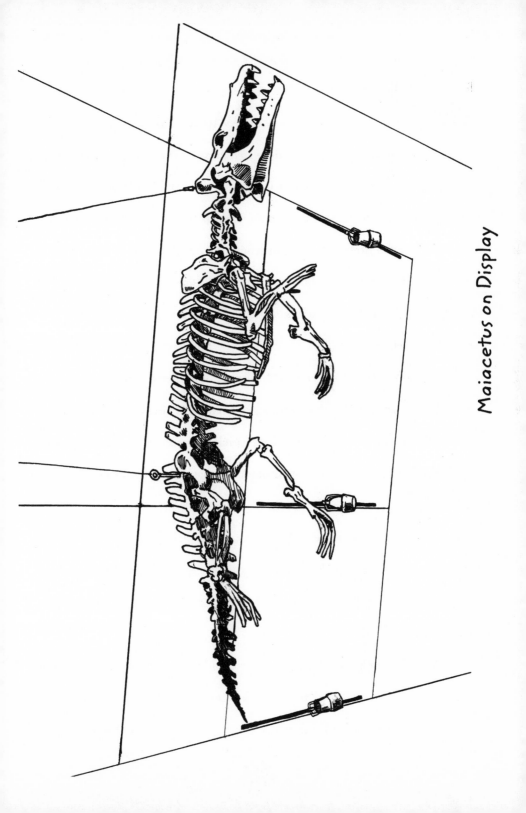

Maiacetus on Display

August 29 — 2:40 p.m.

My time on Orcas Island finally came to a close on Monday morning.

I feel like the last few days re-enacted my first few days on Orcas... a walk

along the beachfront, a boat ride with the Tanners (made just as unpleasant as

the first time with Auntie's tuna sandwiches). We hiked and saw the changes

in the forest from the end of spring to the end of summer. There were fewer

flowers, but the wildlife seemed more prevalent, like it was enjoying the

extended sunlight.

On the same trip, Uncle Pat and Mr. Tanner both tried to teach me how

to track an animal and it almost ended in fisticuffs. Eventually they settled it

with a series of old-man grunts and nods (surely, it has to be its own language),

agreeing the easiest way to tell which way a deer has gone is by the position of its

feces.

Auntie and I went to some of the boutiques and picked out a few pieces of

clothes for my upcoming school year. She treated me to ice cream and one of

her favorite pastimes (that I'm not sure Uncle Pat knew about)—a game of laser

tag.

It's never a good feeling saying goodbye, knowing you won't be returning

for another **year**... That isn't to say I won't enjoy this year in Irvine with

my friends and family, or I didn't miss them while I was here. It's just hard

Orcas Island

to imagine going another full school year without seeing the forests and emerald colors that make up the aptly named Evergreen State. And harder to imagine still: not seeing Charlie, or even the strange Tanner residence every morning.

My bus is starting to pass fir trees. The view outside my window is a reminder I'm not on Orcas Island anymore. The lush greens are  starting to get farther apart, and the grass is longer and lighter and more golden.

As much as I like Irvine, it's going to be a shock to wake up to the scent of burning rubber and the sounds of car alarms rather than bird calls. Not to mention dealing once again with school, something that managed to slip to the back of my mind on Orcas Island. But I'm pretty sure I'll be able to ace biology with little to no effort, and maybe even history, too, if we're talking prehistory.

I do like school, really. It's like a mini city that quits at 3:00 every day. There are social structures and jobs and titles everyone adheres to. I've got friends, sort-of friends, and people I want to punch in the jaw.

I'm thinking about my end-of-year exams more and more. I need to do well on them if I want to get in to University of Washington. (After all, it is right next to the Burke Museum!) I want to be as prepared and well-educated as possible so I can continue working with the Tanners. I don't want Charlie to have to tell me everything all of the time. I learn quick, and I need to be an asset, not a burden.

Ah, Charlie…

We talked about school and the future in our last conversation before I left. Neither of us were sure how the next couple years will play out. It hurt to talk about, truth be told. We wanted to be a soft and sweet couple for the remainder of my time there, but it wasn't practical. That isn't to say we didn't get in some quality boyfriend-and-girlfriend time.

On our last date we went back to the '60s diner. We split a milkshake and enjoyed the irony of being in the past, since that's where we went on our first sort-of date. I asked what his plans for school were, and he said, "We were having such a nice time. Why'd you have to ask that?"

I grinned. "I just wanted to know if you had any plans for prom."

He made a face that was somewhere between amused and perturbed, and his grip on my hand tightened. "You asking me to prom?" He smiled sideways.

"Well, you didn't ask me yet, and prom's only a year away. How ever will I find someone else between now and then?" I joked. "Of course, we'd have to decide which school to go to—"

He cut me off in the middle of my sentence. "Eliza, I'm not attending school this year. I didn't attend last year either. I know it might sound stupid, but I'm getting the training and education I need from my grandfather. My life focuses around taking over the family business, and school had to be cut short because of it." He was looking at the table.

I wonder if he regrets not being able to finish school. I know he rarely sees his parents anymore. He's being primed and trained for this one thing, and it sounds like he's missed out on a good portion of his childhood because of it.

I leaned over and hugged him. "Well, you're not missing much. You'll come to California for my prom them. Problem solved."

I was hoping it would take some of the pressure off, and from the surprised look he gave me it seemed to have worked.

"You still want me to come to prom with you?"

I nodded and said, "It's only junior prom, and I'm pretty sure since I asked you, you're required to wear the dress."

He frowned, and I hoped the mental image I provided him was just as special as intended.

"Don't give me that look, Charlie. You know you love me." I blushed when I realized what I had just said.

"Yeah, I do," he said softly, and we drifted off into an awkward (but happy) silence.

I won't pretend there wasn't a teary-eyed goodbye party inside the bus terminal. Okay, so only me and Auntie were crying. Uncle Pat was grimacing and giving me little knickknacks. He said, "This figurine of a puma carrying deer fawn was created entirely out of Mount St. Helens ash!"

Saying goodbye to Charlie was by far the most awkward. We didn't want to be *romantic* in public, especially in a bus terminal. (Bus terminals are full of very strange life forms, stranger than the ones I studied this summer.) We did the awkward hugging thing, and said, "Uh… you, uh, have email, right? I should get that. For… work-related stuff."

Mr. Tanner shook his head and muttered, "Just like his father."

I can only hope my memories of Orcas Island will be of that last weekend and not the bus terminal. I'd rather remember green isles and laughing faces than the smell of ammonia and broken dreams.

Even as I pass the dry landscape around Mount Shasta at the California border, I'm thinking of evergreens and lapping waves. And if I ever need a reminder of my life on Orcas, I just need to look at the pressed flower now secured firmly to the front of my journal.

Goodbye, Journal.

Mount Shasta

Debut writer Caelyn Aβ Williams was born in Oregon and currently lives near Olympia, Washington. She's had a lifelong interest in paleontology, zoology, and particularly Orcas Island in Puget Sound. She enjoys drawing in her spare time.

Kati Green is an illustrator, fine artist, aspiring drummer, and future tattoo artist. She holds a BFA from the Maryland Institute College of Art in Baltimore, Maryland and currently lives in Portland, Oregon.